NIGHT ON LONE WOLF MOUNTAIN

NIGHT ON LONE WOLF MOUNTAIN

and other short stories

JACK WEYLAND

Deseret Book Company
Salt Lake City, Utah

Library of Congress Cataloging-in-Publication Data

Weyland, Jack, 1940–
    Night on Lone Wolf Mountain and other short stories / Jack Weyland
        p.   cm.
    Contents: Night on Lone Wolf Mountain—Hostage situation—Deck the halls—Jamie's first stand—Prelude to a mission—All we need is a small room—Have yourself a metamorphic Christmas—Quorum lesson number one.
    ISBN 1-57345-113-4
    1. Mormons—Juvenile fiction. 2. Christian life—Juvenile fiction. 3. Children's stories, American. [1. Mormons—Fiction. 2. Christian life—Fiction. 3. Short stories.] I. Title.
PZ7.W538N1   1996
[Fic]—dc20   95-26314
                                                                          CIP
                                                                           AC

Printed in the United States of America
10 9 8 7 6 5 4 3 2 1

To Eleanor Knowles
who, until her retirement as editor and vice president
at Deseret Book, played such a vital role in the
development of many would-be writers.
Without her guidance, always given with gentleness and grace,
many of us would have remained just storytellers
who didn't know when to stop typing.

Contents

NIGHT ON
LONE WOLF MOUNTAIN

Even as Emily hurled the hot pan of burned stew at Shannon, she thought, *This is crazy—I don't do things like this.* Then, because she felt so bad for losing her temper, she immediately began to plan how she'd apologize. Maybe a little note to Sister Ross, the girls camp director. The note would begin, *I really don't know what got into me.*

It was no mystery to everyone else what made Emily blow up. It was Shannon. Some called her Shannon the Shark, although a few objected because it gave sharks a bad name. Shannon had been horrible to everyone from the very beginning of girls camp. She verbally abused other girls, she grumbled whenever she was asked to help, and she talked back to the leaders.

Not that Emily's throwing the pan did any real damage. It easily missed Shannon, and the stew was burned anyway, so there was no great loss. The entire incident might have been forgotten, except for the fact that everyone in camp had seen Emily hurl the hot pan and, also, because it had happened right after another *let's all try to get along with each other* talk by Sister Ross. And with that talk had come a warning to any girls who couldn't get along. They would have to spend the night separated from

1

the rest of the camp at an isolated campsite on Lone Wolf Mountain.

Even though Jeanine Ross sympathized with Emily, she couldn't let what Emily had done go unpunished. She had to carry out what she said she'd do.

Jeanine regretted that Emily was the one who'd finally cracked under Shannon's reign of terror. Emily had never been in trouble before. With her short blonde hair, blue eyes, perky smile, and cooperative attitude she was every adult's ideal youth. Jeanine had heard that Emily actually took notes in Sunday School class and always came up afterward and thanked the teacher for the lesson.

Shannon, on the other hand, appeared to be totally out of control. But that hadn't always been the case. Six months ago, before her older sister Jolene had died in a car accident, Shannon had been fairly normal. But after Jolene's death, she first turned quiet, then sullen. And now she had become belligerent. People had tried to help her get over the loss of her sister, but nothing seemed to work. No matter what anyone did, she seemed to be slipping away. She very seldom came to Young Women activities anymore and almost never to church. Some girls had seen her smoking behind the school.

The adult leaders had been hopeful when Shannon signed up for girls camp. But in the two days they'd been at camp, Shannon had made more enemies than friends. She seemed to take delight in hurting the other girls' feelings.

How can I put Emily on Lone Wolf Mountain with Shannon overnight? Jeanine thought. But that's what she said she'd do, and so she had to do it. The campsite was less than a quarter of a mile away, close enough for her to maintain control, but far enough that whoever was assigned there would know they had been disgraced.

It was time to act. "All right, you two," Jeanine said. "If you can't learn to get along in camp, maybe you can do it outside of camp. I'm sending the two of you to the Lone Wolf Mountain campsite. Maybe you can learn how to get along together up there by yourselves."

"I'm not staying with her," Shannon declared.

Emily was stunned. And she felt like crying. It just wasn't fair.

Jeanine felt the eyes of all the other girls on her. She knew they wanted to see if she'd cave in to Shannon or if she'd stay in control.

"Let me talk to each of you separately," Jeanine said.

Jeanine and Emily took a walk out of camp. "Emily, tell me what happened."

"Shannon burned the stew on purpose."

"Are you sure?"

"I'm sure. I kept telling her to take it out of the fire, but she wouldn't do it."

"Why would she burn the stew?"

"To pay us back for telling her we were tired of doing all the work while she sat around and did nothing except play that stupid video game of hers."

"Is she close to anyone?" Jeanine asked.

"Not really. Not anymore."

"Can you stand to be with her for one night?"

"I don't think so."

"Please try—for me." Jeanine knew it was unfair to ask it that way, but she was desperate.

It was not an easy decision. Emily walked in silence for almost a minute before finally shrugging her shoulders, sighing, and saying, "Well, all right."

Jeanine patted her on the back. "I knew I could count on you."

"That's what I'm here for," Emily said quietly.

Her remark puzzled Jeanine.

A short time later Jeanine walked the same path with Shannon. "You're not very happy here, are you?"

"Duh, what was your first clue?" Shannon said.

"You don't have to take that tone of voice with me."

"It's the only tone of voice I've got."

"Really? How unfortunate." Jeanine had to remind herself to stay focused. Shannon brought out the worst in her.

Shannon was a good three inches taller than Emily. Her dark, thick eyebrows could have added to her beauty but now only served to accentuate her perpetual scowl. Since March, Shannon had worn her hair cut razor short along the sides. It was what the rebel girls at school did. Shannon apparently hadn't decided for sure what she wanted to be because it was long enough on top that she could cover over the sides. The way she did her hair was a barometer of how rebellious she was feeling. Today, the longer hair was swept back to show off the sides.

She has everything a girl could want except a good attitude, Jeanine thought. *I wonder what she looks like when she's sleeping, without the scowl, without the muttered disapproval of what anyone in authority says, and without the cruel jokes at others' expense.*

"What happened back there?" Jeanine asked, trying not to sound judgmental.

"You saw it."

"Emily's usually not the type that blows up like that."

"Are you saying it was my fault?" Shannon challenged.

"I didn't say that, did I?"

"No, but you were thinking it."

"So you're completely blameless in all this?"

"That's right."

"Really? Emily says you purposely burned the stew."

"So—are you going to believe Twinkle Toes instead of me?"

Jeanine had to fight the urge to grab Shannon and shake her. She took a few deep breaths. "What can we do to make you happier while you're here?"

"Nothing. I never should have come. The only reason I did was because my mom bribed me. She promised me a shopping trip if I'd go to girls camp. I can hardly wait to go buy me some new clothes. Boys really seem to like me in halter tops and tight jeans."

"Sometimes you say things to try to shock people, don't you? I mean, that's why you mentioned the halter tops and tight jeans, isn't it? Because you knew I wouldn't approve."

"No. I said it so you'll know I've had it with church and people like you. I won't be coming back anymore. As soon as my mom comes to pick me up on Saturday, you'll never see me again."

"What have we done to make you so bitter?"

"Nobody here likes me."

"And you think that's our fault?"

"Look, let's just get this over with, okay?"

"All right, just tell me why you and Emily were fighting."

"I like to try to make her mad at me, except that most of the time she doesn't fight back. Usually she acts like if I'm mad, it's her fault. She's such a doormat—usually, that is. I mean, I was surprised as anyone when she hauled off and threw the pan at me."

"Shannon, I need your cooperation. I told everyone what I'd do if there was any more conflict. I need to have both of you go to the camp on Lone Wolf Mountain. I have to send you both."

"I'd rather be sent home than be with her. She puts up

this big front like she's so perfect. Sometimes I want to knock on her forehead and go, 'Hello? Anybody home?'"

"Maybe you could help her."

"Yeah, right. Like I could cut her hair, so it's like mine."

Even Jeanine smiled at the thought of Emily with shaved sides.

"I need your help, Shannon. Please go along with this and spend one night on Lone Wolf Mountain with Emily."

Shannon thought about it, then turned to Jeanine. "All right. Go ahead. Play it for all it's worth. I'll go along with it. Of course, once I get back I might tell everybody it's all your fault I quit going to church. I mean, I got to blame somebody, so it might as well be you. But you'll know it's not you, so don't let it worry you if that's what you hear coming back."

"I hope you'll change your mind about church."

"Forget it. It's not going to happen."

*   *   *

An hour later Emily and Shannon hauled their equipment up the hill to the campsite on Lone Wolf Mountain. Everyone watched them go. Officially, at least for that night, they were outcasts.

By the time they made it to the campsite, it was six-thirty.

"You planning on getting any sleep tonight?" Shannon asked.

"Yes, why?"

"If I were you, I'd try to stay awake."

"Why?" Emily asked.

"Because it'd be a shame to fall asleep and wake up with all your hair cut off."

"You wouldn't do that."

"Wouldn't I? Don't count on it." Shannon sat with her back up against a tree, her head down, playing a video game on her Game Boy.

Emily emptied the canvas tent bag onto the dirt. The aluminum poles clattered as they hit the ground. She was hoping that would be enough of a hint so that Shannon would offer to help.

"We need to set up the tent," Emily said.

"Why?" Shannon answered, not even looking up from her game.

"In case it rains."

"It's not going to rain."

"Well, then, for privacy."

"Who are you afraid is going to see us? Chipmunks?"

Emily unfolded the tent. "You're not going to help out at all, are you?"

"Why should I? You're the one who wants to set up the tent, not me."

Emily turned away and mumbled something.

Shannon stood up and approached. "Excuse me, what did you say?"

"Nothing."

"No, you said something. Was it about me? Because if you've got something you don't like about me, just say it to my face."

"All right, I will. I said I can see why people talk about you at school."

"You think I care what people say? Besides, you should hear what people say about you."

"What do they say?" Emily asked.

"That the only reason you get good grades is because after class you're all . . . " Shannon began a mean-spirited imitation of Emily: "Oh gosh, Mr. Anderson, you're such a good teacher. I just can't believe how much I'm learning in this class. Is there any extra reading I can do?" Shannon glared at Emily. "How can you do that day after day and still have any self-respect left?"

"I know this will be a new thought to you," Emily replied, "but some people like to learn."

"Yeah, right," Shannon scoffed, "and others just like to chum up to their teachers."

"Look, I really don't want to talk about this anymore," Emily said. "Besides, we need to get everything set up. And let me tell you something, Shannon—if you're not going to help out, then I'm definitely not setting up the tent all by myself."

"You think I care? Why can't we just ignore each other while we're here?"

"Fine, but don't blame me if it rains and you end up getting all wet," Emily said. She sat on the tent and wrote in her journal while Shannon played her video game. As the sun neared the western tree tops, Emily looked around. "We need to fix something to eat while there's still enough light."

"I'm not hungry," Shannon said.

"You're just saying that because you want to get out of work."

"I'd help if I was hungry, but I'm not, so you go ahead if you want."

Emily picked up a can opener. "Oh, I see. You figure you'll let me do the cooking, and after it's ready, you'll suddenly decide you're hungry and I'll give you some. Well, that's not going to happen. I mean it. Whatever I fix is for me. You're not getting any of it."

"Fine."

Emily stood up. "I'm going to get some kindling now for a fire."

"Why do you always talk like you think you're better than everybody else?"

"What are you talking about?" Emily asked.

"Everybody else'd say, 'I'm going to get some sticks to start a fire.' Not you, though. Oh, no, you've got to hit me with the word *kindling*."

"Kindling isn't just sticks, Shannon. Kindling can be dried pine needles. So if I said I was going to get sticks, and ended up bringing back pine needles, then you'd probably tell me that pine needles are not sticks. Well, I know that, Shannon. I know what a stick is, and I also know what kindling is, so I'm going to get some kindling now, which can be either sticks or pine needles. There, now are you satisfied?"

Shannon shrugged her shoulders. "Yeah, whatever."

"You could help out, you know."

"I could, but I'm not going to," Shannon said.

"Why not?"

"Because I've got a bad attitude. Ask anyone. They'll tell you."

"Listen to me—I'm not your personal slave. If I start a fire, then it's my fire, not only for now but for the rest of the night, and no matter how cold it gets, it's still my fire."

"I don't need your fire, and I don't need your cooking," Shannon said.

"I can see now why they threw you out of camp."

"They threw you out, too, you know."

Emily paused. "I know, but that was a mistake."

"A mistake? What are you talking about? You threw a hot pan at me."

"You were supposed to watch the stew so it didn't burn," Emily said.

"I watched it for a while."

"Then how come everything got burned?"

"Somebody must have put some more wood on the fire when I wasn't looking."

"So you weren't watching after all, were you?" Emily said, claiming a small victory.

"If that's what you want me to say, then fine, I'll say it."

"You can sit there all night playing that stupid game, but you'll be sorry you didn't help me get *kindling*." She used the word as a weapon.

A few minutes later, she returned. "I'm back."

Shannon looked up from her game. "I thought some bear got you. I was trying to decide what to put on your tombstone. I finally came up with, '*She went to get kindling and never came back.*'"

"Go ahead, make fun of me, but when it's cold, you'll beg me to let you sit by the fire, and you'll plead with me to give you something to eat, but I'll just laugh in your face. I'm serious, Shannon. This is your last chance. Are you going to help me or not?"

"No."

"All right, then. Have it your way." Emily started a fire, opened a can of beans, poured it into a pan, and set the pan on the fire. She took great care to keep stirring it so it wouldn't burn. She even picked out each tiny piece of ash that fell in.

At last it was ready. She ate it out of the pan, making as many noises of appreciation as she could for Shannon's benefit. She wanted to eat it all to spite Shannon but could finish off only about half of what was in the pan.

Shannon looked up from her video game. "You got any left?"

"A little."

"Can I have some?"

"You know perfectly well what I said about that," Emily said.

"I know, but I was just thinking—if you're not going to eat it, anyway, it wouldn't be right to waste it. Besides, I am kind of hungry now."

Emily sighed. "All right, here." She went to hand over the pan.

Shannon wouldn't take it. "What is wrong with you anyway? Why would you even think about giving me something to eat when you said you weren't going to do it? Why do you always give in? Do you think you have to be nice all the time? You make me sick."

"But you said you wanted some."

"What difference does it make what I said? I can't believe how you let people walk all over you. Don't you have any self-respect? For once in your life why don't you stick up for yourself?"

Emily didn't know what she should do with the pan of beans, to give it or to take it back. "Do you want this or not?"

"I already told you I didn't want any. And you told me I couldn't have any. So let's just keep it that way. And the next time you say you're going to do something, then stick to it. Don't cave in all the time. That's one of the main reasons people at school don't respect you."

Emily was devastated. "People don't respect me?"

"Not the people I run around with. They make fun of you all the time."

"Why?"

"All this year you've let Chelsea copy your science homework. Right?"

"Once in a while."

"Don't give me that—you let her copy it every day. She makes a copy and gives it to Chad, who gives it to everybody on the football team. And from there it goes to the girls' and boys' basketball teams and then to the cheerleaders and then to anybody else who wants it. As far as I can tell, you're the only one in school actually doing any homework. You're like the school joke. That's why people break out into big grins when you walk by. You probably thought it was because you're so popular, right?"

Emily's lower lip began to quiver. "Chelsea and everybody else are taking advantage of me?"

"Yeah they are—big time. Haven't you ever wondered why Chelsea ends up in all your classes? Sorry I had to be the one to tell you. Well, come to think of it, I'm not sorry. Actually, I enjoyed it, if you want to know the truth."

Emily sat down and pouted.

*   *   *

Jeanine Ross tried to eat something at dinner, but she wasn't hungry. She was too worried about Emily being with Shannon overnight with no adult supervision. What if Shannon went after Emily with a knife? Or decided to do a prank that ended in tragedy?

Jeanine knew she had gone beyond what anyone would say was reasonable. *It's going to be a long night*, she thought. *I know I'm not going to get any sleep. If I have to, I'll stay up there all night to make sure nothing happens to Emily. This was a dumb idea. I never should've said I'd send troublemakers to Lone Wolf Mountain. What if some man comes along and finds the two girls all alone? Or if a bear gets them? It could happen. And if it does, whose fault will it be? It will be mine. I've really messed up this time.*

She felt a comforting hand on her shoulder. It was one of the other adult leaders. They'd both been going to girls camp for ten years.

"They'll be okay," she said.

"Sure they will," Jeanine said, not really believing it. She decided that after it turned dark, she'd sneak up and see how they were doing.

*   *   *

As the darkness began to close in, Emily looked around for something to do. She decided to get ready for bed. Her sleeping bag had been in the family a long time. A few rips had been patched and the drawstrings that used to go around it had long ago pulled out. Now it was held together by two black bungee cords. Because Emily didn't want to risk losing them, she had neatly written her name on them in white ink at one end. She undid the bungee cords. "Where should we sleep?"

"Anywhere you want," Shannon said, still playing her video game.

"If we had a tent set up, then I'd know, but the way it is now, I could put it any direction."

"It really doesn't matter."

"I know, but could you set yours down? Then I can make mine parallel to yours."

"What is wrong with you anyway? Our sleeping bags don't have to be parallel."

"I know, but that's the way people usually have them."

"So? For once in your life, live on the edge."

"Put yours down first, okay? Please?"

"I can't believe this," Shannon fumed, standing up, grabbing her sleeping bag, untying it, and flinging it down on the ground. Then she sat back down and resumed her game.

Emily put her bag down parallel to Shannon's. "I think it's better if they're parallel. That way we can talk."

"We can still talk if our sleeping bags aren't parallel."

"I know, but it's better if they're parallel."

"Why?"

"I don't know. It just is. It's more like we're together if our sleeping bags are parallel."

"Parallel sleeping bags—I bet you did well in geometry, didn't you?"

She nodded her head. "I did all the proofs."

"The entire school thanks you for doing 'em, too, Emily. We all owe our grades to you."

"I'm the one who learned though."

"Like anyone at school cares about that."

"I care."

"Then you're the only one."

Emily decided to ignore Shannon's negative attitude. "I heard this logic puzzle before I came up here for girls camp. See if you can figure it out. A little boy and a little girl are sitting on a park bench. 'I'm a boy,' the one with black hair says. 'I'm a girl,' the one with red hair says. Okay, now here's the puzzle—if at least one of them is lying, which is which?"

"Did you get a look at 'em? I mean, it's not that hard to tell a girl from a boy."

"I know, but the thing is, you don't have to see them to figure it out. You can use logic."

"Are you crazy? Why would I use logic for that when I can just look at someone and tell if they're a boy or a girl? I mean, where exactly is this going to come in handy?"

"Don't get mad at me just because you can't work it out. There're a lot of things I can't do as well as you."

"Like what?"

Emily had to think about it. "You're really good at intimidating people."

"Thanks a lot."

"Well, it's true. Look, I can explain the thing about the

boy and the girl to you if you want. The one who says she's a girl is actually a boy and the one who says he's a boy is actually a girl."

"Why would two little kids lie about something like that?"

"I don't know. It's just a story problem, okay? See, the thing is, you know that at least one of them is lying. Okay? So, suppose the boy is lying and the girl isn't. Then they'll both say they're girls, right? Or if the girl is lying and the boy isn't, then they'll both say they're boys. They can't both tell the truth, either, since we know at least one is lying. So the only other possibility is that both of them are lying. Do you get it?"

"Do you actually go around with worthless garbage like this in your head?" Shannon asked.

"Yeah, pretty much."

"No wonder you're so messed up. Get a life, okay?"

"I have a life."

"Yeah, you do. You're a people pleaser. That's what your life is all about, isn't it?"

"Well, no one could accuse you of that, that's for sure," Emily said.

"That's right. I'm my own person." She shook her video game. "Just my luck, I'm stuck out here with you all night, and my batteries are dying on me."

"I really think we should set up the tent."

"Look, let's get a few things straight. I'm not going to help you set up the tent, I'm not hungry, I don't want to tell ghost stories, and I don't want to sing songs around the campfire. I especially do not want to look up at the stars and talk about how long it's taken the light to get to us. There, does that pretty much cover it? So just leave me alone. Is that asking too much?"

"The way you're acting, leaving you alone will be a pleasure."

"Fine, then do it."

Emily spent the next half hour gathering firewood. Once she got it into the campsite, she arranged everything into three piles: one pile for kindling, one pile for medium-sized pieces, and one pile for large chunks from downed trees.

Shannon was the first one to break their silence. "You still got any of that pork and beans left?"

"Yes."

"Can I have some?"

"Are you serious? After the way you treated me? No way."

"Forget what I said before. I'm really hungry now."

"There's another can," Emily said. "Gather some firewood, start a fire, open the can, put it in a pan, and cook it yourself."

"Okay, look, maybe I was a little hasty in what I said about you never standing up for yourself. Now let me have some of your leftovers."

"No way." Emily picked up the pan with the leftover beans in it and moved away from Shannon.

"Don't make me take it away from you, Emily. I'm a lot meaner than you are."

Emily let out a large sigh, smiled, and said, "I don't think so." She tossed the pan out into the darkness. They could hear it hit the ground and then clatter down the hillside.

"Are you crazy? What did you do that for?"

"Am I letting people walk all over me now? Huh? Is that more like what you wanted?"

"You just threw away our only pan!"

Emily pursed her lips. "Oh, yeah. Sorry. Well, we'll look for it in the morning."

"In the morning? How am I supposed to cook anything without a pan?"

"That's the least of your worries, Shannon. You don't even have a fire to cook over. This is my fire. This is my kindling pile, this is my medium-sized wood pile, and this is my big-sized wood pile. If you want to make a fire, get your own kindling. Oh, excuse me, get your own *sticks*. And don't build it near my fire either."

"Don't make me beat you up."

"Like you could."

"How many fights have you ever been in?"

Emily paused. "Plenty."

"Don't lie to me. You never even get angry."

"I do, too. I yelled at my little brother once."

"How come?"

"He wrote on a report I was supposed to hand in the next day."

"What did you say to him?" Shannon asked.

"What difference does it make?"

"Just tell me what you said."

"I said, 'I really wish you hadn't done that.'"

"You call *that* yelling at your brother?"

"He knew I was mad at him by my tone of voice," Emily said.

"You don't have a tone of voice, Emily. You go from sweet to sickening sweet."

"That's not true."

"Oh no? Try saying something mean to me," Shannon dared.

"No."

Shannon held her hands out and gave a *let me have it* gesture. "C'mon, give me your best shot."

"I don't want to say anything I'll regret later on," Emily said.

"Say something to get back at me. Say something really mean."

"All right! You asked for it! I really think you should spend more time on personal hygiene."

"That's it? That's the best you can do?"

"Yes, and now I'm really sorry I said it."

"C'mon, say something to set me off so we can get into a fight."

"You want to fight me?" Emily, wide-eyed, asked. "I bet you learned about fighting from those cowboys you run around with."

"That's right," Shannon said. "At least they let you know what they're thinking, so they're a lot better off than you." She came up and deliberately pushed Emily backward a few inches.

"You can't do that," Emily said.

"Why can't I?"

"Because you just can't."

Shannon pushed her again. "There. I just did it again. What are you going to do about it? Why don't you unleash your logic skills on me, huh? That's your big secret weapon, isn't it? Let's see—how would that go? Two girls are camping out in the woods all by themselves. One of them is lying. The first one says that life sucks. The other one says life is good. Which is which? Hit me with your logic, Emily! That's about all you got going for you, isn't it?"

Emily stood there, looking at Shannon. "You never used to be like this. What happened?"

"It's none of your business what happened. Are you going to fight me or not? Because if you don't stand up for yourself, you'll get hurt a lot worse."

"Are you this way now because your sister died?"

"Stop right there. Nobody talks to me about her."

"I'm sorry she died, Shannon."

"That's it! I warned you, but you wouldn't listen. Now we have to fight. You don't stand a chance against me 'cause I'm taller and meaner and know more about fighting than you'll ever know."

"There are other ways we can settle this without fighting."

"Like what?"

"Well . . . we could arm wrestle," Emily said.

"Arm wrestle?"

"Sure, why not? I think I could beat you at that."

"There's nothing you could beat me in."

"Except arm wrestling," Emily said confidently.

"Fine, then, we'll arm wrestle."

Emily took care of all the arrangements. She searched around the woods until she found the stump of a tree that someone had cut down. If they knelt on the ground and faced each other, it would be perfect for arm wrestling. She cleared the ground around the stump and brushed away most of the ants that called the stump their home.

Suddenly Shannon screamed.

"What's wrong?" Emily called out.

"I just stepped on a snake!"

"Where?"

"Right here."

Emily went over to investigate.

"How come you're not afraid?" Shannon asked.

"I've taken every life science course at school, that's why. Besides, this is the problem." She bent down and picked up one of the bungee cords from her sleeping bag. "You call this a snake?"

"You put that down there on purpose, didn't you?" Shannon said.

"Yeah, right. Look, I think I've got everything ready now. We probably should bring our sleeping bags so we'll have something to kneel on."

"What for? It's not like it's going to last that long. It'll all be over in a couple of seconds."

"Don't be so sure of that. Remember one thing, Shannon. I play the violin, so my right arm is pretty strong. You try bowing through one of Beethoven's symphonies sometime and see what it does to your arm muscles."

"Like I'm really scared." Shannon went over to the tree stump. "Why'd you pick here? The place is crawling with ants."

"You'll just have to live with it. I didn't see you trying to find a place."

"All right, let's get this over with."

Emily carefully folded her sleeping bag in thirds, placed it on the other side of the stump, and then, still standing, began to blow out air and then suck it in again with a kaa-sound.

"Excuse me," Shannon muttered, "but what are you doing?"

"Breathing exercises. Mr. Foster taught it to us in choir. Proper breathing is very important for any activity—even arm wrestling."

Shannon threw up her hands and paced back and forth. "Why can't we just fight like normal people? Why does everything have to be such a big production with you?"

"I'm ready now." Emily kneeled down, facing Shannon. She put her right arm on the stump as did Shannon. "Okay, now. How this works is on the count of three . . . one . . . two . . . th—" Just before she finished saying *three,* Emily slammed Shannon's arm down on the stump and jumped up to celebrate. "I won! I won!"

Shannon stood up to protest. "You cheated! You started too early!"

"I started on three."

"You started on *th*!"

"The *ree* was silent. Besides, you're just a sore loser."

"Let's do it again, and this time I'll be the one who counts," Shannon said.

"Sorry, but that's it. We're done fighting for the night. Face it, you lost."

Shannon brought her face within inches of Emily's face. "I want a rematch, and I want it now."

"I know you do, but you're not going to get it because, well, to tell you the truth, I kind of hurt my arm, so I'd better not do it again because I've got a concert next week. We're doing Mahler."

"Something else, then."

"Well, all right, I suppose we could try leg wrestling. Have you ever done that? I used to do it with my brother when we were kids. I was good at it, but that might be because he let me win. You want to try it?"

"Anything, as long as it will end up making you hurt all over."

"You really ought to work on that bad attitude, you know." Emily went and got their sleeping bags and brought them back to camp. She laid them out parallel. "Okay, what we do is lie down on our backs, side by side, and we go one, two, three, and then we put one leg up in the air, and we lock legs and try to dump each other over. Okay?"

"You don't have to explain everything to me all the time. I'm not dumb, you know."

It was dark by now, but the fire gave them enough

light to see. They both lay down, side by side. "Oops, this isn't going to work," Emily said.

"Why not?"

"Because when I dump you, you'll end up rolling into the fire. Let me just move the sleeping bags a little."

Emily chose another location and then lay down to test it. "Nope, this isn't good either. I've got a rock digging into my shoulder. I think we'll have to move again."

Emily ended up moving the sleeping bags two more times before she was satisfied. "Okay, I think this will work out."

"All I wanted was to fight you, but no, with you around we'll end up putting on the Summer Olympics." Shannon got in the position for leg wrestling.

"Okay, you ready?" Emily asked. "One . . . "

"Stop right there!" Shannon interrupted. "I'll do the counting this time, thank you very much."

"If you want to count, go ahead. It won't make any difference in how it turns out."

"One . . . two . . ."

"Look, a shooting star!" Emily said excitedly.

Shannon wasn't buying that. She didn't even bother to look. With one lunge, she flipped Emily over and then got up so she could gloat in Emily's face. "You thought you could fool me with that, *Oh, look, a shooting star*, didn't you? Well, I'm not that dumb."

"I wasn't trying to trick you. There *was* a shooting star. And because I was distracted, it wasn't fair. I know I can beat you. Let's do it again."

They agreed to the best out of seven. By the fourth time, though, they were both laughing too hard to continue.

As their laughter subsided, they lay on their backs,

staring up through the canopy of trees. Shannon finally said, "There are a lot of stars out tonight."

"I was just thinking the same thing."

They were quiet for a few moments, gazing up through the pines at the stars above them.

"Do you think maybe Jolene is up there someplace?" Shannon asked.

"Maybe so."

"Do you think she can see me now?"

"I bet she can."

Shannon got up and sat down by the fire. She was quiet for several minutes, staring into the flames. "Jolene was a lot like you," she finally said.

"Oh, she was much better than I'll ever be."

"I miss her."

"I do too," Emily said. "When I started Young Women, she was the only one of the older girls who came up and talked to me."

"It's not fair," Shannon said, staring into the fire.

"I know. It isn't."

"If I could just know for sure that she's okay, then that would make it easier."

"She is okay, though. You know that, don't you?"

Shannon sat up. "No, that's just it, I don't."

Emily came over and stooped down and rested her hand on Shannon's shoulder. At first Shannon stiffened but then gradually she relaxed.

It wasn't until Shannon wiped her face with the sleeve of her denim jacket that Emily realized Shannon was crying.

"You okay?" Emily asked.

"I don't know why I'm doing this," Shannon said. "I didn't cry when I first heard about Jolene, and I didn't cry at the funeral. So I don't know why this is happening now."

"It's okay, though, really. You've been through a lot."

"I loved her so much, and now she's gone, and there's nothing I can do about it."

"I know, but at least she's with Heavenly Father," Emily said.

"Are you sure about that?"

"I really am, Shannon."

Shannon nodded. "I'm glad you know that. I wish I did."

Shannon stood up and walked away from the fire, staring into the darkness. She finally spoke. "Can I tell you the things I remember about Jolene?"

*   *   *

Jeanine Ross moved up the trail. It was slow going in the dark. She had used her flashlight until the last turn heading up to where the girls were camping but turned it off so they wouldn't see her coming.

Girls camp meant more to her than she ever let on. She and her husband had five boys. They were wonderful, but she missed not having a daughter, so every year these girls became her daughters. She loved them all. Even Shannon.

She stumbled and fell over a tree root in the trail, banging her shin on a rock as she landed. She stayed on the ground and rubbed her leg to try to take away the pain. *This is insane,* she thought. *I think I'm losing it. I'm getting too old for this. I don't have good judgment anymore. If Shannon or Emily's parents find out what I did, they're going to be furious with me. I don't blame them either. Sending them up here by themselves was a bad idea.*

She looked up the trail. She could see the light from the girls' fire now. Just a few more steps and she'd find out how they were doing. If things were out of hand, she'd bring them down for the night.

As she drew closer, she saw Emily and Shannon sitting next to the fire, talking.

They're okay, she thought. She decided to return to camp and check back a little before midnight.

*   *   *

"Thanks," Shannon said. "I feel better now. In fact, I think I'm actually hungry. I think I'll cook up that other can of beans."

"I can help if you want."

"No, I can do it. Just help me open this can will you? I'm not used to this kind of can opener."

"Sure." Emily opened the can and handed it back to Shannon.

"Thanks." As Shannon took the can from Emily, they made eye contact. "I know I've made you think I didn't like you," Shannon said, "but that's mainly because I didn't want to be around anything that reminded me of Jolene. The truth is, I sometimes wish I could be more like you. You've got your faith in God, and you live the way you're supposed to, and you're always happy."

"You need to keep stirring the beans or they'll get burned on the bottom."

"Yeah, okay, thanks."

Emily got up and dropped one of the large pieces of wood on the fire. It landed with a thud, and sparks rose up into the black sky. She looked upward and watched them, each one eventually losing its red glow. "I'm not really the way I'd like to be," Emily admitted.

"I guess nobody is."

"I guess not," Emily said. She watched Shannon stir

the beans. "How come you never come to Young Women anymore?"

"Jolene went all the time and look where that got her."

"If she could talk to you, I bet she'd tell you to go."

"She probably would, but I'm thinking it's probably too late for that now, anyway."

"Why would it be too late?" Emily asked.

"Because I've got such a bad reputation now. And when I do end up going, the other girls look at me like *what is she doing here?* They never talk to me, either. But that's not the worst of it. At school the girls from our ward never say hello. To tell you the truth, I don't think I'm ever going to go back."

"I say hello when you come to church."

"I know, but you always have *perfect* written all over you. So I always figure you do it mainly because you're supposed to. You don't talk to me at school, either."

"That's because you're always with your own friends," Emily said.

"You could still say hello."

"Well, maybe so, but actually, your friends scare me."

"They're not that bad. Really. They just look scary."

"Why don't you go with me to Young Women? I could pick you up each week. We could hang around at school, too."

"I don't think so."

"Why not?"

"You know I smoke, don't you?" Shannon asked.

"Well, yeah, I've heard that."

"You really don't want to go out in back and smoke with me and my friends during lunch period, do you?"

"No, not really."

"I didn't think you would. In school, if people even

saw us eating together, they'd say you were really going downhill."

"I wouldn't care," Emily said.

"Yeah, sure, like I believe that. The way it looks to me, that's all you do care about."

Emily paused, "You know, Shannon, people can change. Maybe even me."

"It probably wouldn't hurt me to spend some time with you, either," Shannon said. "Maybe some of your perfectness would rub off onto me."

Emily shook her head. "I really don't think you'd want that to happen."

"Why not?"

Emily moved away from the light of the fire. She was on the verge of saying something she'd never admitted to anyone before.

"Is something wrong?" Shannon asked.

"No, I'm fine. I just got some smoke in my eyes is all."

Shannon got up and went to where Emily was standing in the shadows. "Something is wrong, isn't it?"

"No."

"Don't lie to me. I didn't lie to you."

Emily turned around to face Shannon. "Okay, I won't lie to you. The fact is that sometimes I'm scared."

"What are you scared of?"

"I'm scared—of me."

"Is this another one of your screwy logic problems? Because I really don't understand why you'd be scared of yourself."

"I have to be in control all the time. And everything has to be perfect—everything—my grades . . . my makeup . . . my hair . . . my homework . . . my weight. And I have to be nice all the time. I can't get mad because it wouldn't be perfect. I have to be happy all the time. Except, I don't always feel happy. Sometimes I feel like a rubber band that keeps getting stretched tighter and tighter. And someday it'll break. There're things I do now that I never used to do that I don't tell anyone about . . . like one day I went to make a cake when my mom and dad were gone, and when it came out of the oven, it had split down the middle, so I threw it away because it wasn't good enough."

Shannon couldn't help smiling. "Seriously? You threw away a cake? You should've called me. I'd have taken care of it for you."

"I throw everything away that isn't perfect. Like, I think I threw you away, too. After Jolene died, I knew you were having a hard time, and I kept thinking I should try to be your friend, but then you started running around with that other crowd. You were just like the cake, so I let you go because I was afraid people would talk about me if I went out of my way to spend time with you. I'm not very proud of that."

"Don't be so hard on yourself all the time."

"That's what I need to stop doing all right. The last week of school I got a 98 on a test and went in to argue for the two points. The teacher finally gave them to me, just to get rid of me."

Shannon folded a sweatshirt into a few layers and used it to remove the can of beans from the fire. She grabbed a spoon and took a bite. "This tastes great. Want some?"

"Yeah, I really would."

"Grab your spoon and let's go to it."

They bent over opposite sides of the can and took turns spooning out the beans. At one point Shannon looked over at Emily and noticed her cheek had a black smudge on it and there was a bit of bean juice running down her chin. That's when she knew she was good for Emily.

After they finished eating, Shannon asked Emily, "Have you ever stayed up all night?"

"No."

"What do you say we do it tonight?"

"Why?"

"Because we're bad," Shannon said.

Emily's eyes got big. "We are?"

"We are."

"Okay, but bad doesn't really mean *bad*, does it? Because I don't want to be bad in a bad way, if you know what I mean."

"What do you want to be?"

Emily thought about it. "Well, actually, I'd settle for normal."

"Okay, if you really want to be normal, then you got to prove it by doing a girls camp prank."

"You want me to do a prank?"

"Yes, that's what normal people do. Can't you think of something?"

"Well . . . we could clean out all the fire grates, so when everybody gets up they'll wonder who did it."

"Hey, look, we're not Keebler elves here, okay? How about if we pour syrup on all the toilet seats?"

Emily made a face. "I don't think so. Too messy. But what if we secretly made little pinecone key rings for all the girls?"

"You really need some help on this, don't you?"

"Looks that way."

"Maybe this will help us get into the mood. Let's both smudge our cheeks with some charred wood from the fire and tie bandannas around our heads."

"Well, why not?" Emily said with a silly laugh.

After Shannon finished with Emily's face, she looked at her and said, "All right, we're stylin' now. Next thing we gotta do is a prank. Just think of this as a big test in school, and one of the questions is that you have to come up with a really good idea for a prank. I'll help you with all the details, but the main idea has to come from you."

"My very first prank," Emily said, sounding both excited and nervous at the same time.

"I can give you a couple of ideas to get you going. There's the one where we run the adult leaders' pants up the flagpole. Or the one where we put honey in all the shampoo. Or we sew somebody's sleeping bag shut during the day."

"Any of those would be good," Emily said. "The only problem is they don't affect everybody in camp, and they don't last long enough. I'm sure we can do better than that."

Half an hour later, when their plan finally emerged, Shannon said, "That is really bad, Emily."

Emily smiled. "It is, isn't it?" And then from Emily's perfect smile came a low, throaty laugh that nobody had ever suspected was there.

*   *   *

At six o'clock that morning Emily poked her head in the leaders' tent. "Sister Ross, there's something we need to talk to you about." Shannon stood nearby.

"What's wrong?"

"Well, Shannon and I wanted to do a prank, and I was so excited because it was going to be my first prank, but then something went really wrong and, well, we thought maybe you should know about it."

"What happened?"

"Well, we thought it would be fun to put a snake in one of the showers, you know, to scare the girls. So we caught a water snake this morning, and we put it in the shower, but . . . well, now this is the part we didn't think about . . . we're pretty sure the snake went down the drain. Not only that, but we think it's still down there. I really feel terrible about it."

"But don't worry," Shannon said. "We're pretty sure we can catch it if it comes out."

Sister Ross sat up, now fully awake.

"We were thinking it might come out when the girls are taking showers because of all the water," Emily said.

"We've already gone to every tent and told everyone, so they'll be on the lookout while they're taking a shower," Shannon said.

"Which shower stall did you put the snake in?" Jeanine Ross asked.

"That's just it," Emily answered. "We can't remember. It was kind of dark, and we were in a hurry."

"And all the drains are connected to one big pipe," Shannon said.

"So there's no telling which drain the snake will decide to come out of."

"But don't worry," Emily said. "It was our mistake this even happened, so we'll do whatever we can to fix the problem. Shannon and I will be outside with a shovel while everyone is taking their showers," Emily said. "So whatever drain the snake decides to come out of, we'll rush in there and catch it before it goes back again."

By ten o'clock that morning no girl in camp had even tried to take a shower. A few of the braver ones had used the small washbasin to wash their faces, but nobody wanted to spend much time in that building.

"This is stupid," Jeanine Ross announced to the girls during lunch. "A little snake isn't going to hurt you."

"Then how come you haven't had a shower, either?" one of the girls asked.

Nobody took a shower that whole day. It gave Emily and Shannon plenty of time to fasten one end of Emily's bungee cord inside the drain of one of the showers. They tied the other end to some light fishing line. When they tugged on the fishing line, the bungee cord would wriggle out of the drain. When they let go, it snapped back inside the drain. With water running, to someone paranoid about snakes, it would be pretty convincing.

The next day, at the flag-raising ceremony, Jeanine Ross looked around. The girls looked awful. Their hair was stringy and matted down, their faces all smudged with dirt. Ordinarily that would not have mattered much, but tonight all the parents were coming to the annual girls camp talent show. Jeanine did not want the parents to see their daughters looking so grubby. "This is absolutely ridiculous," she began. "Every one of you will take a shower this morning. I will not have your parents seeing you looking this way."

"What about the snake in the shower?" one girl asked.

"I'm sure that snake has left long ago. Snakes do not live in drainpipes. To prove it, all the adult leaders will take their showers first. After we're done, the rest of you will follow."

Emily and Shannon waited until the adult leaders were in the showers, then they went to the shower building and pulled the fishing line until the bungee cord came out of one of the shower drains.

A woman's scream could be heard throughout the entire camp.

And then Emily let the bungee cord snap back into

place. That meant the snake was still at large. Except for Emily and Shannon, that was the last shower taken that day.

By five o'clock, the parents of the girls began to arrive. Shannon and Emily were the only ones who looked halfway decent. The other girls looked like they'd been raised by wolves.

After supper and halfway through the talent show, one of the fathers, who happened to be a plumber, returned to the group. Sister Ross had asked him to check out the shower drains.

Between skits, Jeanine asked in front of everybody, "Did you find anything?"

"Yeah, I found this in the drain." He held up the bungee cord.

"It says here that it belongs to Emily Stanton."

"Emily?" Jeanine asked.

"Oh, gosh, you found my bungee cord!" Emily, sweet-faced, said. "Thanks a lot! I was wondering where it'd gone."

"Nice try," Shannon whispered.

Jeanine Ross knew then that they'd been had. "Shannon and Emily, is this the snake you were telling us about? You tricked us, didn't you?"

Emily was hardly able to control her pride. "Yes, we did it!" she blurted out, "but it was my idea! My very first prank! It was a good one, too, wasn't it? I mean, it kept all of you from taking a shower for two days. My gosh, I hate to say anything, but you all look awful!"

Jeanine felt the eyes of all the parents on her. How would she react? Would she be dignified? Would she be fair? Would she show the proper decorum?

No, not really. This was her last girls camp. If she was going out, she was going out in style. "Get them!" she shouted. "Let's throw them both in the shower!"

Shannon and Emily tried to get away, but there were too many and they both ended up in the shower with their clothes on.

"Boy, you sure got us!" Emily said as she and Shannon returned to the campfire after changing into dry clothes.

"Not as bad as what you did to us," one of the older girls said.

"And we're not done yet, either," another girl threatened.

Because it was their last night at camp, Emily and Shannon asked if they could spend it on Lone Wolf Mountain. Jeanine Ross could see that some good was coming out of this, after all. "All right, but no tricks."

*   *   *

"I can't believe we got away with it," Emily said as they arrived back at their campsite on the mountain.

"I knew we would," Shannon said. She enjoyed being street-smart for Emily.

"They might still come for us tonight," Emily said.

"If they do, we'll be ready."

"What about after camp is over?" Emily asked.

"What about it?"

"I don't want to go to Young Women alone. Who knows what those girls might do? They're still pretty mad about what we did."

"You still want me to go with you?" Shannon asked.

Emily nodded her head. "I think we're going to need to stick together for a while."

Shannon nodded her head. "I guess maybe that'd be okay."

"At school too?" Emily asked.

"They probably won't try anything at school."

"I know that, but I need you to help me."

"What can I do?" Shannon asked.

"Well, if you'd been with me that day I got that test back, you'd have told me it was stupid, since I already had a 98, to go in and argue for two more points. And you'd clue me in to quit letting people copy my homework. And you'd tell me it's okay to get mad once in a while."

"You want me to say things like that to you?"

"Yeah, I do," Emily said.

Shannon shrugged her shoulders. "Well, sure, I guess I could do that."

"Okay, it's settled then."

"You might be able to help me too," Shannon said.

"How?"

"I need to quit smoking."

"You just need to set a goal and then work at it. I can help you with that."

"Also, I need someone to keep telling me that everything is going to be all right."

"It is, Shannon. It really is."

As Shannon slipped into her sleeping bag, she had to tease Emily. "Boy, it's sure a good thing these things are parallel."

Five minutes of small talk and then Emily said, "We forgot to say our prayers."

"Do we have to?"

"You always have to say your prayers."

A long pause. "Okay."

"We should get out of our sleeping bags and kneel."

"I just got my sleeping bag warm."

"You don't kneel when you pray at night?"

"All right, I'll kneel, but this is as far as it's going to go, right? I mean, you're not going to have us build an altar out of stones or anything like that, are you?"

"No, it'll be just kneeling."

There was a long pause while Shannon wrestled with the idea. "You'll just keep after me until we do it, won't you?"

"You got it."

"All right, we'll pray then," Shannon said with an air of resignation as she crawled out of her sleeping bag.

After their prayer, they lay back down and looked at the stars and talked about God and Jolene and life.

It was their last night on Lone Wolf Mountain.

HOSTAGE SITUATION

7:45 A.M., February 1

It was cloudy and cold with a threat of rain as Josh Davis entered the high school. He'd gotten up too late again to say his morning prayers. He felt bad about it because today was Friday, and on Tuesday, when he'd met with the bishop, he'd finally admitted he was thinking about not going on a mission after all.

"Why wouldn't you go?" the bishop had asked.

"I've been planning on going, but after we won the state title in football, I got a lot of phone calls from different colleges. And, well, I've had an offer to play for Nebraska. One of the coaches there said he thought I could be the starting quarterback by my sophomore year. When I told him I was thinking about going on a mission, he told me he didn't want me unless I could guarantee I'd be there for the next four years. So that's a problem. The thing is, I'd really like to play for Nebraska."

"There must be some other college you could play for that'd let you go on a mission after your freshman year and then come back and play."

"Maybe, but Nebraska was number one last year. If I play for Nebraska, it could be my ticket to the NFL."

Bishop Reynolds shook his head. "Josh, you've really taken me by surprise. You've always planned to go on a mission. When do you have to declare your decision to Nebraska?"

"I told them I'd let 'em know on Monday."

"You'll pray about this, won't you?" Bishop Reynolds had asked.

"Well, yeah, sure."

"I'd like to meet with you Sunday after church to find out what you've finally decided."

"Okay." Josh stood up to leave. "Thanks, Bishop."

"I'll see you on Sunday, Josh. Be sure to pray." He looked intently into Josh's eyes. "I mean *really* pray."

And now it was Friday, and he hadn't prayed. Of course he'd joined in with family prayers, and he'd even offered quick prayers by his bedside each night, but he hadn't done what the Bishop Reynolds wanted him to do. He hadn't gone to his room and closed the door and knelt down and taken time to pray for help to make the right decision.

And now it was Friday.

9:30 A.M.

Harlan Quentin slept until after his stepfather left for work. His mother had been out of town for almost a week and the house was a mess. The kitchen sink was full of dirty dishes and something in the refrigerator smelled awful. There had been no reason for Harlan to get up because he'd been kicked out of school the day before.

There was one teacher especially responsible for him being kicked out of school. Mr. Adams had been down on him from the first day he entered his class. He had made fun of Harlan for his long hair and the old, black topcoat he wore most of the time.

Harlan hadn't done anything wrong except for missing quite a few days of school and not turning in much of the assigned work. It wasn't right to be kicked out of school just for that. Somebody needed to pay for what they had done to him. Especially Mr. Adams.

Harlan didn't know what was going to happen to him. He'd never gotten along very well with Bill, his stepfather, a no-nonsense construction worker who had no use for Harlan's appearance or what he called Harlan's "downright laziness." His mother and Bill weren't getting along very well, either. His mother had been gone for six days. She said she needed to take care of a sick aunt, but Harlan wasn't convinced that was the real reason and wondered if she'd ever come back. If she didn't, Harlan knew it wouldn't be very many days before Bill would throw him out. He didn't know what he'd do then.

Harlan went into the bathroom. He turned on the tap and splashed his face with water. As he dried his face, he looked at his reflection in the mirror. A few whiskers sprouted from his chin and his eyes were sunken and had dark circles under them. His face was broken out again, and his long hair was greasy-looking. *I'm ugly,* he thought. And it made him angry.

When Harlan went downstairs to look for a box of cereal, he noticed Bill's gun case. He opened the glass door and pulled out a hunting rifle and sat in front of the TV and sighted in on a talk-show host and pretended to blow him away. The gun was empty. Harlan went to the gun case and found a box of shells.

A few minutes later he stood in the living room and pointed the gun through the window at a man walking his dog. It made him feel powerful. The feeling was exhilarating, but it was also scary.

Harlan set the rifle down. His heart was racing. He sat down again in front of the TV, but he couldn't concentrate on the program.

He remembered how Mr. Adams had looked when he kicked Harlan out of class. He had sneered at Harlan and acted like he'd won some kind of victory to finally get rid of him. It had been unfair and humiliating. *What would it be like,* he thought, *to bring a gun into Mr. Adams's classroom and make him get down on his knees and beg for his life and apologize for what he'd done.*

But it wasn't just Mr. Adams who needed to be taught a lesson. It was everyone else in the class too. They all turned up their noses and never talked to him. He knew they laughed at him and made fun of the way he dressed. They all needed to be taught a lesson—today.

11:09 A.M.

A misty rain had begun when Harlan entered the school. He was wearing the long, black topcoat he'd picked up at the secondhand clothing store for a dollar. It was long enough so that with one hand inside the coat, he was able to conceal the rifle.

Harlan was proud of himself for thinking of everything, even to the best time for him to show up at the school. The halls were nearly empty, just as he knew they would be. The first lunch period would begin in ten minutes.

Nobody stopped him. He opened the door to Mr. Adams's classroom and stepped inside.

Mr. Adams looked over at him and scowled. "You're not in this class anymore, Harlan. You're not even a student here. I thought I made that clear yesterday."

Harlan smiled. "I decided to come back anyway. I have a little surprise for you today, Mr. Adams. I guess you could say it's my version of *Show and Tell*." He brought the rifle out from inside his coat and pointed it at Mr. Adams. "Say good-bye to the class, Mr. Adams."

Mr. Adams looked shocked, but, even so, he still

sounded like a teacher as he said, "Put that away, Harlan. You can't have a gun in here. It's against the rules."

"It doesn't matter what the rules say because with *this* I make all the rules. I want you to get down on your knees, Mr. Adams. I want you to beg me to spare your life. Who knows, maybe if you use good sentence structure, I might not kill you. But it'll have to be very good, Mr. Adams. I'll tell you that right now."

Deciding that it was him and not the students that Harlan had come for, Mr. Adams moved slowly toward the back of the room. There were two doors, one at the front of the room, the other at the back. Mr. Adams hoped to get close enough to either door to make a run for it. As he backed away, he held up his hands with the palms open toward Harlan. He lowered his voice. "Don't do anything foolish, Harlan. Whatever problems we've had in the past, we can work them out. There's no need for any violence."

Harlan moved menacingly toward Mr. Adams.

Josh Davis sat in the back row, unable to do anything but look on.

With Harlan near the back of the room, Mr. Adams moved to the side of the room the doors were on and began backing toward the front of the room. "Harlan, look, I have two kids. Do you want to see a picture of them? If you kill me, they won't have a father."

"Like I care."

"Just look at the picture of my kids, Harlan. Here, I'll show you. I have a picture of them in my wallet. Just look at it. That's all I ask. Here." He took his wallet out of his pocket and handed it to a student who in turn passed it to the person behind him.

"Why should I want to look at your kids? I don't care about them. I don't care about nuthin'."

"Please, just look at the picture, that's all I ask," Mr. Adams said.

The wallet made it to Harlan. It was sitting on the desk next to him.

Mr. Adams waited, then said, "The oldest is Tiffany. She's ten years old. The youngest is Brett. He's seven. Please just look at them. Is that too much to ask?"

Harlan reached down and picked up the wallet but kept his eyes on Mr. Adams.

"Just open it up. The picture is right there."

Harlan could see nothing wrong with looking at Mr. Adams's kids before he made him beg for his life. He opened the wallet and glanced down.

That was all Mr. Adams needed. He bolted for the door. Harlan dropped the wallet and brought the rifle up and fired just as Mr. Adams reached the door. The noise in the confined classroom was deafening. A girl screamed.

The bullet splattered into the metal casing around the door just after Mr. Adams made it out into the hall. Harlan ran after him, yanked open the door, and looked both directions down the hall, but Mr. Adams had disappeared around the corner.

Harlan slammed the door shut and stomped to the front of the classroom. The girl who had screamed was crying hysterically. No one moved to comfort her. The rest of them sat there, every one of them, staring dumbly at Harlan, hearts pounding, eyes wide open.

Harlan felt a surge of excitement. He saw the fear in their eyes. He loved the feeling of power he had discovered. Nobody was making fun of him now.

Josh looked around the room. Everyone was too scared to do anything except stare at Harlan to see what he'd do next.

To Josh it was more than just the deafening sound of a

rifle being fired in a closed space that had paralyzed them. Before Harlan walked into the room, school had always been a safe place, but, now, that feeling was gone forever.

Josh was the only senior boy in the room. He should have taken the class when he was a sophomore, and he'd signed up for it then. But because football took so much time, he'd had to drop it. He'd postponed taking it his junior year because he was embarrassed to take a U. S. history class where everybody else was a year younger than he was. Finally, in his senior year, it had come down to the fact that if he didn't take the class, he wouldn't graduate.

He wasn't really afraid of Harlan. Josh was taller, stronger, faster, and more disciplined than Harlan would ever be. He knew that if he could get close enough, and if he could somehow distract Harlan, he could take the gun away.

Josh looked around the room for someone who might help him. Over half the class members were girls. Of the boys, all of them were sophomores. Some of the boys, especially, seemed too young to even be in high school.

He'd just have to wait for the right time.

Harlan rested the butt of the gun on a desk, with the barrel pointed straight up. He leaned forward and said, "If you all do exactly what I say, then maybe nothing will happen to you today. But you cross me once, and you'll pay for it—big time." He smiled. "So, it looks like it's just us then, doesn't it?"

The only girl who'd ever gone out of her way to say hello to Harlan said, "Let us go, Harlan. We never did anything to you."

"I'll let you go, but not just yet. I want Adams and the principal to think about what I might do. Let 'em sweat it out for a while. But don't worry, I'm not going to hurt anybody if you all do what I say."

A girl on the first row got up to leave.

"Where do you think you're going? Sit down!" He moved quickly toward her.

She sat down. "Please let me go. I'm not feeling very good. I think I'm going to be sick."

He walked over to her and said in a low, threatening voice, "If you feel bad now, think how bad you'll feel with a bullet through you."

She closed her eyes. "Please don't hurt me," she pleaded.

Harlan looked around. Everyone was looking at him with what he took to be respect. *They don't know what I'm going to do,* he thought. *It's like they're my toys, and I can do anything I want with them.* He loved the feeling it gave him— a feeling of power he'd never felt before. He was in control now, and they all knew it.

"Will you be good?" he asked the girl. Even to him it sounded strangely out of place, like some frustrated baby-sitter trying to get a little cooperation. Except that it wasn't the way he felt. He had the power. He knew that. But, also, he wanted them to like him. That's all he'd ever wanted.

"Yes," the girl whispered. Perspiration was beaded up on her forehead, and she held her hand to her mouth.

Harlan smiled. "Okay, then I won't kill you. Just be good." He walked to the front of the room and addressed the class. "You guys look worried. Don't be so afraid. This is going to be fun. I mean, this is what we've always dreamed about, isn't it? School without teachers. This doesn't have to be a bad experience, as long as everybody does exactly what I say. Nobody can leave. I'll shoot any-body who tries, okay? We all have to stick together, right? One big happy family."

Looking around the room, Josh decided there was only

one person he could trust to have a cool head under pressure, and that was Brooke Jennings. She was a senior who played on the girls' basketball team. From the games he'd watched, Josh knew she could maintain her composure, even in a close game.

"Can I go to the restroom?" a girl asked.

"Nobody leaves," Harlan said.

"Please let me go. I can't hold it."

"If you try to leave, I'll have to kill you, 'cause if I let you go, then pretty soon everybody will want to go, and nobody would come back."

"We'd come back," another girl said.

"No you wouldn't. Nobody here likes me. I don't have a single friend in this entire stinking school. You all think you're too good for me, don't you?" He began sweeping the gun wildly in front of him. They all froze, afraid to even breathe for fear it would set Harlan off.

"Well, don't you?" Harlan pressed. "The only reason you're here is because I've got a gun. You'll be my friends as long as I've got a gun on you, but the minute I let my guard down, it's all over and then I'll know how much you've hated me all along."

Glaring angrily, Harlan scanned the class for any movement. He began to pace back and forth. "Well, I'll tell you one thing, I'm sick of it! Do you hear me?" he shouted. "I'm sick of school! I'm sick of people who don't give other people a chance just because they don't wear fancy clothes or they don't have the right parents. I'm sick of my life. You think I care if I live or die? Well, I don't! I don't care! It doesn't matter to me. In fact, it'd be better to be dead because once you're dead, that's it. So I'd better start getting a little cooperation around here. You understand? You can either give me a little respect voluntarily, or else I'll make you do it. And I can do it, too. See that clock. You

want me to show you what'll happen if any of you step out
of line!" He aimed the rifle at the clock and pulled the
trigger. A girl screamed and pieces of glass showered the
people closest to where the clock had been. "*That's* what
will happen if anybody steps out of line!"

The intercom crackled. "Is this on?" they heard someone say. A pause and then, "Harlan, this is Officer Burton
of the police department. I'd like to talk to you for a
minute if that's okay with you."

Harlan treated it as a joke. "Well, sure, Officer Burton.
What would you like to talk to me about?"

"We heard a shot a minute ago. Is anyone hurt?"

"Not yet. I was just showing what'll happen if people
get out of line."

"I see. Okay, well, we were just wondering. Harlan, I
really think we can work this all out if you'll just put the
gun down and come out in the hall. I'll meet you halfway
and personally guarantee that nobody will hurt you. This
hasn't gone too far. I think we can resolve the situation to
everyone's advantage." The pitch of his voice was low, and
he spoke slowly.

"Well, that's very interesting, Officer Burton. Thank
you for sharing your thoughts with me because now I
know what you're thinking. Would you like to know what
I'm thinking, Officer Burton? Would that be of interest to
you?" He pointed the rifle at what was left of the clock
and fired again.

"Stop it!" a girl cried out. "I can't stand this anymore!"

"Shut up!" Harlan screamed.

"Harlan?" Officer Burton said.

"What!"

"We can work this out. Just tell me what you need."

Harlan's attention was drawn away from the girl and
back to Officer Burton. "Listen to me, Burton, if you send

anybody down the hall or make a move on us, I'll open fire, and I won't miss, either. You'll be carting bodies out of here all day. And don't think I won't do it, because I will. I've got nothing to lose."

"We'll stay back, Harlan. Don't worry about that."

"You'd better."

"Anything else?"

Harlan thought about it and then smiled. "Yeah, sure, bring us some pizza . . . and something to drink. We're going to have a party."

"What kind of pizza would you like, Harlan?"

"Just a minute, I'll find out." He spoke to the class. "What kind of pizza do you guys want?"

Everyone was too terrified to say anything.

"I said, 'What kind of pizza do you want?'" He approached Jason Richards on the first row. "Jason, what kind of pizza do you like? You get to pick. Whatever you want, okay?"

"I'm not very hungry."

"We're going to have a party, Jason, so you got to tell me."

Jason shook his head. "I don't care. Any kind."

"No, I have to know!" Harlan shouted. "What kind of pizza do you like? Tell me!" He struck Jason across the side of his face with the gun barrel.

"Pepperoni," Jason said quickly, holding his face.

"Pepperoni it is, then!" Harlan said cheerfully before moving on to Natasha, again on the front row. "What kind do *you* like?"

Natasha had learned her lesson. "Supreme."

"All right! Supreme!" He cocked his head back slightly in the direction of the intercom. "You getting this all down, Officer Burton?"

"We got pepperoni and supreme."

"Can we have some Dr. Pepper too?" Natasha asked.

Harlan beamed. "Yes, of course! Natasha is getting into this big time! She doesn't mind partying with me, do you, Natasha?"

Natasha knew a few things about manipulating boys. "Are you kidding? Free pizza and drinks? That beats what we usually do in here. Harlan, you're my man. I'm serious."

Still beaming from what Natasha had said, Harlan spoke to everybody. "Now you see? That's the way I want all of you to be. You think I like ordering you around? Well, I don't. What's going down here today is as much for you as for anyone else. I mean, let's face it, the system's corrupt, and we all just got to stay together, and if we do that, we can make it through this or anything else. I'm not the bad guy here. The whole system is rotten. I know I don't have to tell you guys that."

Officer Burton's voice came over the intercom. "Harlan, I've ordered ten pizzas and two cases of Dr. Pepper. It'll be here real soon."

"Sounds good."

"We just want you to take it easy, Harlan."

"Right, I'll bet you do. Now I want you to turn that thing off, Burton. I don't want you listening in to what goes on here. We can hear when it's on, too, so don't try to be clever."

"I'm turning it off now, Harlan. I'll contact you, though, when your pizza gets here." There was a click and the intercom went dead.

Harlan lowered the gun so it wasn't pointing at any of them. "Now look, you guys, let's make this a real party. Let's put all the chairs into a circle, except I don't want anybody behind me. And, Natasha, I want you to pull the black curtains down so nobody can see what we're doing in here. And also, Natasha, put something over the windows in the doors so nobody can see in. Then we can do anything we want. So everybody get into a circle. And don't try anything, or I'll have to start shooting."

"Whatever you say, Harlan, whatever you say," Natasha said.

Harlan noticed a girl sitting in the back of the room, wearing a cross on a chain around her neck. She had her eyes closed and was mouthing a silent prayer. He walked quickly back to her, grabbed the cross, and yanked it off her. "You don't need that. I'm not going to hurt you. I'm not going to hurt anybody . . . not as long as everybody does exactly what I say."

"How long are we going to be here?" a girl asked.

"I don't know."

"A long time?"

"Maybe. But it'll be okay because we got everything we need . . . a TV . . . food . . . so it'll be okay. Just think of it like we're all at a party at my place."

"It'd be easier to relax if you'd put the gun down," Natasha said.

Harlan's festive mood vanished. "No. I got to have the gun because if I put it down, you'll all run out of here. If I really did have a party, none of you would come. Don't say you would, either, because I know better."

Josh sat and waited and watched Harlan switch back and forth from being their executioner to being their friend.

Half an hour later Officer Burton's voice came over the PA system. "Harlan, your pizza is here. You want me to send the delivery guy down to you with it?"

"How stupid do you think I am, Burton? You'd send some cop wearing a Domino's uniform. Did you really think I'd fall for that?"

"Harlan, my job is to resolve this situation peacefully. I'd never try some dumb plan like that because it could get people hurt. My hope is that we can get through this without any bloodshed. This guy really does work for Domino's. He's right here. You can talk to him if you want."

"I said no, didn't I?" Harlan screamed in rage.

"All right, don't get upset. Just tell me what you want me to do."

"I don't know."

"Harlan?" Josh called from the back of the room. "If you want, I'll go get it."

"If I let you go, you won't come back."

"No, I'll come back. I promise. I'd have to come back for Brooke anyway." Josh had been to a party once with Brooke, and they'd talked. He was hoping she'd go along with whatever he said.

"Are you two going together?" Harlan asked.

"Yeah, we just started, but we're talking about getting married as soon as we graduate," Josh said.

Brooke caught on and played the game. "Don't worry, Harlan, he'll come back, 'cause if he doesn't, he'll be in big trouble with me."

It was a lie, but Josh thought they might get away with it because Brooke and he were both seniors, and Harlan was only a sophomore and totally out of it as far as knowing what was going on.

"And that's the worst kind of trouble to be in," Josh said with a forced smile.

Harlan considered it for a few moments. "All right, you can go, but if you don't come back, then Brooke will be the first one."

As Josh walked past Brooke to go to the front of the room, she asked quietly, "You are coming back, right?"

"Yeah, I'll be back."

"Good."

Harlan turned on the intercom. "Burton!" he called out. "I'm sending somebody to get the pizza. Have it on a cart in the middle of the hall. He'll pick it up and bring it to us."

"Sounds good. I'll tell you when we're ready."

"No, no. I don't want you ready. I want you off balance. Listen to me, you got two minutes. If you're not done by then, you can just forget the whole thing."

"I need a cart, pronto!" Burton called out to someone just before switching off the intercom.

The girl who had asked to leave to use the restroom timidly raised her hand.

"What?"

"Can I go with Josh to get the pizza? I'll come back." She closed her eyes. "Please, I really need to use the bathroom."

"I'd like to help you, but who would I shoot if you didn't come back?"

"Nobody."

"Oh, no, I'd have to shoot somebody. I mean, after all, those are the rules."

"Please, please let me go," she started sobbing.

"Sorry. I guess you're out of luck."

Officer Burton came back on the intercom. "Harlan, we've got everything on the cart. We're going to do like you said and push it halfway down the hall and leave it there, and then you can send someone to get it."

"No tricks, Burton."

"No tricks."

"If this doesn't work out, then I'm going to have to start shooting people and throwing bodies out into the hall. And it'll be all your fault. So don't get any big ideas."

"We're going to play this straight, Harlan, because I need you to trust me."

"All I'm saying is, you'd better not try anything."

"We're ready for you now, Harlan. Enjoy your pizza."

Harlan nodded to Josh, who moved slowly toward the door. His heart was pounding and breathing was difficult. He knew that he was setting himself up to be shot if Harlan took a sudden disliking to something he did.

Harlan pointed the gun toward Brooke. "You know what'll happen if you don't come back, don't you?"

"I know. I'll be back."

"He'll come back, Harlan," Brooke said. "He'll come back for me."

Harlan seemed satisfied. "All right, go get our pizza so we can party."

Josh turned to make sure Harlan wasn't about to shoot him, then opened the door and started down the hall. The school looked deserted. Through the windows of a classroom, he saw a large crowd of people outside and several police cars.

He came to the cart. There was a police officer hidden in the recessed doorway of a nearby classroom. "How many guns does he have?"

"Just one. It's a rifle."

"An automatic?"

"I don't think so."

"Has he reloaded since he's been in there?"

"No."

"How many shots has he fired?"

Josh had to think about it. "Three."

"What exactly does he want?"

"I'm not sure. Look, I've got to go now. He'll shoot Brooke Jennings if I don't go back." He put his hands on the cart and then, almost as an afterthought, he said to the police officer, "I might try to stop him."

"Don't do it. Let us handle it. It's too risky for you to try anything."

"What can you do?" Josh asked.

"Burton might talk him into giving himself up."

"I don't think so. Look, I've got to go now. Harlan gets spooked easily."

"We have sharpshooters posted outside, if you can get him to open the curtains. And we have a SWAT team on the roof. So don't you try anything dumb."

It'll only be dumb if it doesn't work, Josh thought as he pushed the cart down the hall, trying to make up for lost time.

"Father in Heaven, please help me," he mouthed the words.

When he opened the door, he forced himself to smile. "I got the pizza, guys. Let's dig in."

"Nobody move!" Harlan angrily shouted at the top of his voice, then turned his rage on Josh. "You think I don't know what's going on?" he screamed. He had the rifle pointed at Josh's midsection.

Josh backed away from the cart with his palms turned up so Harlan could see he didn't have a weapon. "What are you talking about, Harlan?"

"You were gone too long. I don't know what it is, but you've cooked up something with the cops. Haven't you?"

"No."

"Don't give me that! There's something going on!" Harlan brushed his long hair back out of his face.

"Like what?"

"I don't know, but there's something wrong. This was too easy. Like maybe the pizza's been poisoned or has something in it to put everybody to sleep."

Josh shrugged his shoulders. "It's just pizza, Harlan. That's all it is."

"I don't think so. Let's see you eat some of it."

Josh forced himself to smile. "Sure, Harlan, whatever you say."

He picked up one of the boxes from the cart and set it on the teacher's desk. He opened the box and took in the aroma. "Oh man, that smells good, doesn't it?" He picked up a piece and took a bite. Speaking with his mouth full, Josh said jokingly, "You know, Harlan, I think you're right. I think it is poisoned." He eyed the cases of Dr. Pepper on the lower shelf of the cart. "The Dr. Pepper is probably poisoned too. How about if I try some to find out for sure?" He wanted it to sound as though he was teasing.

Harlan glared at him and then a slight smile crossed his face.

"Sure, go ahead."

Josh opened a can and took a big drink. "Yep, this stuff is definitely poisoned. Boy, it's a good thing we found out about it." He finished off the slice of pizza, wiped his mouth with a napkin, smiled, and picked up another slice. "You know what? This is just about the best poison I've ever eaten."

"It's not poisoned," a girl said.

"Okay, okay," Josh said, "so maybe this one wasn't. But that might be because it's pepperoni. You know what? I bet they poisoned just the supremes. Maybe I'd better try a couple of slices of that. What do you think, Harlan?"

Harlan couldn't help smiling. "Yeah, maybe so."

Josh made a big deal out of finding one of the supreme pizzas, setting it out on the desk, picking the biggest slice he could find, and showing how much he enjoyed each bite. In reality, because he was so nervous, it tasted like cardboard. "Definitely poisoned. Maybe I should try another pepperoni."

"Hey, save some for us!" Brooke called out. "Harlan, don't let him hog it all, because he will if you let him."

"Don't listen to her, Harlan. You were right all along. I'd better sample every one of these pizzas, just to be on the safe side."

Harlan had lowered the rifle so it was no longer pointing at anybody. He turned to the class. "You see what I mean? This doesn't have to be bad for everybody. You think I like scaring people? Well, I don't. I just want a little respect, that's all."

"Harlan, would you like me to set the pizzas out for everybody?" Josh asked. He decided that to build trust he should call him by name as often as possible and ask permission for every little thing. "If you want me to, I can set 'em along the table by the window; then people could just get up and go get a piece."

Harlan nodded. "Yeah, go ahead."

Josh pushed the cart over to two long tables that ran alongside the windows. He set out each box and opened it. The last thing he did was set up cans of Dr. Pepper beside each box of pizza. "I think we're ready, Harlan, unless you want me to sample another pizza."

"Okay, we've got to do this a few people at a time," Harlan said. "Okay, you three can go."

Within a few minutes everybody was eating pizza. Josh, still standing, moved closer to Harlan. "They're having a good time, aren't they? I think everybody appreciates you getting this for us. I'll tell you one thing, Harlan, this sure beats going to class."

"It is good, isn't it? I just want everybody to have a good time, that's all. That's all I've ever wanted for us today."

"I think they know that now, Harlan. There is one thing that'd make this perfect though," Josh said.

"What?"

"Well, we're going to be here for a while, aren't we?"

"Yeah, we'll be here a long time."

"That's what I thought. The problem is that after everybody goes through all the Dr. Pepper, we're all going to really need a bathroom."

"I can't have people leaving here. If I let them, they'll never come back."

"You let *me* go, and I came back."

"That's only because you knew that Brooke would be wasted if you didn't come back."

"Would you really have shot her, Harlan?" Josh asked.

"I think it's important that when I say I'm going to do something, then I should do it."

"So you would've killed her?"

"I'd have shot her but maybe not killed her. Maybe I'd have just shot her in the leg or something like that. Why do you want to know?"

"Just curious, that's all. Knowing you'd go after her, though, wasn't the only reason I came back."

"What other reason did you have?"

"Are you kidding? I could smell the pizza, and I just wanted to be with my friends—like you, Harlan."

"Are you my friend?" Harlan asked.

"Well, we haven't been, but I think we could be."

"I don't have very many friends."

"I think you will from now on."

"Do you think so?"

"Sure. If nobody gets hurt, then this'll be the one day at school where we all got to do whatever we wanted."

Harlan looked pleased. "You understand then, don't you? I just want everyone to be happy, that's all."

"I know you do, Harlan. And I respect you for that."

"But if it doesn't work out, I'm not going to let them put me in jail."

"What will you do?" Josh asked.

"I'll take care of it, that's all. I'm not going to have people making fun of me anymore."

"Things will work out, Harlan, I'm pretty sure."

"Maybe. We'll just have to see."

"Anyway, like I was saying before, I think you and I should try to see if we can somehow rig up a bathroom in here. What would you think about that?"

"Like how?"

"Well, we could move the desk over to that corner and turn it up on its side to give people some privacy. And then we could put a chair back there and a wastepaper can. And we could open the window by the corner a little bit to let some air in, I don't know, what do you think? I could pretty much do it all. It'd only take me a couple of minutes."

"Why do you want to do this?"

He leaned closer to Harlan and spoke confidentially. "To tell you the truth, Harlan, I really need to use a bathroom myself."

Harlan smiled, then nodded his head. "All right, go ahead."

"Thanks. It'll just take me a minute."

He's letting me move around, Josh thought. *Now all I have to do is look for my chance.* He slid the desk to the front left corner of the room, turned the desk up on its side facing out, then set a chair and the wastepaper basket behind the desk.

"Harlan, this isn't much good. How about if I drape part of the curtain over the desk to just give people a little more privacy."

Harlan seemed relieved to have somebody helping him. "Okay, but I don't want somebody getting a clear shot at me through the window."

"I'll be careful." He noticed Harlan wasn't eating. "Harlan, you want me to get you something to eat?"

"I don't know."

"I really don't think they've put anything in the pizza. Do you?"

Harlan looked around at everyone who was eating. "All right, I'll take some."

"You want something to drink, too, Harlan?"

He nodded his head. "Okay."

Josh felt the same kind of anticipation he did before a game. Things were going his way. All he had to do was keep a clear head and wait for the right moment. He thought a quick prayer like he sometimes did just before a game began. He opened two cans of Dr. Pepper, grabbed a couple of slices of pizza, and carried them over to where Harlan was standing. "Here you go," he said.

"Thanks."

"No problem, Harlan. This is really turning out okay, after all. Everybody seems to be having a good time. You suppose we could play some games after everyone's done eating?"

"I'm not very good at games."

"I'll take care of it. Oh, and one other thing, we should probably get our order in for supper, so they have plenty of time to get it for us."

"Good idea."

Josh took a big swig of drink and then burped. "You ever chug-a-lugged a can of Dr. Pepper? It's impossible to do without burping before you finish." Josh moved six inches closer to Harlan. He was now close enough to touch him with an outstretched hand.

"I can do it."

"I don't think so, Harlan. Nobody can do it. I've tried it. It's totally impossible."

"I've done it before," Harlan said.

"No way!"

"I have. Really."

"You want to have a contest just between you and me? We both start with a full can. The first one done without burping wins." *C'mon, Harlan, take the bait,* Josh thought. "Or how about this? The first one to finish a slice of pizza and a can of Dr. Pepper without burping wins. There's no way you'd ever beat me on that, Harlan. No way."

"I could beat you," Harlan said.

"You think so, huh?"

"I'm sure of it," Harlan said.

"Well, maybe we should find out for sure."

"All right."

"How about if we ask Brooke to be the judge?" Josh asked.

"That'd be okay."

"Is it okay if I have her come up here, Harlan?"

"Okay."

Josh made an announcement. "Listen up, everybody, Harlan and I are going to have a race to see who can finish a can of Dr. Pepper and a slice of pizza without burping. And Brooke's going to be the judge. Brooke, you want to come up here?"

Brooke picked out two nearly equal slices of pizza. She handed one to Josh and held the other out to Harlan. As Harlan reached to take it from her, Josh lunged forward and wrenched the rifle away from Harlan. It slid along the floor. As Harlan dove for it, Josh tackled him from behind and grabbed his arms. "Everybody out!" Josh shouted.

Everyone started shouting and bolted for the doors.

"One at a time!" Brooke cried out.

As the room emptied, Brooke turned to Josh. "You need any help?" she asked.

"No, go get the police. I'll hold him until they get here. Hey, Brooke, thanks. I knew I could count on you."

She shrugged her shoulders. "Yeah, sure, no problem," she said before leaving the room.

Harlan was laying on his stomach with Josh sitting on top of him. Josh turned him over and straddled Harlan, sitting on the smaller boy's stomach and holding Harlan's wrists, pinning him to the floor. "Don't move, Harlan, or I'll have to beat you up."

"I thought you were my friend," Harlan said.

"Are you kidding? You're a loser. What if you'd killed somebody?"

Josh felt a surge of anger. It infuriated him to think of Harlan waving the loaded rifle at the class. Then Josh suddenly shuddered and realized he was shaking.

Harlan lay still. He seemed devastated. He looked so vulnerable lying there on the floor, his hair in his eyes, his topcoat awry.

"Would you do me a favor?" Harlan asked.

"What?"

"Could you shoot me?" Harlan said it as if he were asking for a piece of gum.

"What? You want me to shoot you?"

"Yes, please."

Hearing Harlan say that, Josh began to feel a little bit sorry for him. "I'm not going to shoot you, Harlan."

"Why not? You could say that after everybody left I went for the gun and you tried to stop me and we fought and then the gun went off. Please. I don't want to live anymore."

"Why not?"

"What's there to live for?"

"Lots of things."

"Not for me. You were right about me. I am a loser."

"Okay, look, Harlan, I shouldn't have said that. I'm sorry. What I should have said was—"

Suddenly, two policemen burst into the room with their guns drawn.

"We'll take over now," one of them said to Josh.

Josh looked up. They looked mean.

As he stood up, Josh said, "Don't hurt him, okay?" One of the policemen rolled Harlan over onto his stomach, yanked his arms backward, and handcuffed him.

"Hey, take it easy," Josh complained.

They were a little more gentle as they helped him to a standing position and then escorted him out of the room.

It was over. Josh looked around the empty classroom. It was a mess: the overturned desk, empty pizza boxes, soda pop cans, spilled drink, glass from the shattered clock. He went out into the hallway and was met by Officer Burton. "You must be Josh Davis."

"Yeah."

"The students told me what you did." He shook Josh's hand. "Good job."

"Thanks."

"Your parents are outside waiting for you. They've been here since the very beginning. We couldn't let the parents inside the building, so they had to stand in the rain."

The families and students were milling around in the rain, hugging each other. Some of the kids were crying and there was a lot of confusion. Josh's mother and father saw him as he walked out of the building. His mom ran to him. "Oh, Josh." She held Josh in her arms. Since the eighth grade he had towered over her.

"I'm okay."

His father came up from behind and put his arm around him and squeezed. "We were so worried. All we could do was pray."

"We kept hearing shots, and we didn't know what was happening," his mother said. "I didn't know if you were alive or dead."

One boy and his parents walked over to where Josh was standing with his mom and dad. Josh didn't even know his name or anything about him except that he was a sophomore and didn't say much in class. The boy had been crying and said to Josh, "Hey, man, I just want to thank you for what you did."

"What did you do?" Josh's mother asked.

The boy answered, "He took the gun away and wrestled Harlan to the floor and told us all to leave. If it weren't for him, some of us would probably be dead by now." The boy's voice cracked.

Josh saw the look of alarm on his mother's face. He tried to minimize what he'd done. "I didn't do that much really. And Brooke Jennings helped me."

The boy's father reached out and shook Josh's hand. "Thank you for saving our son's life."

Josh was embarrassed to be the center of attention. "I was just lucky, that's all."

"That was great what you did," the boy said.

The boy's mother added, "Thank you for my son."

Josh put his hand on the boy's shoulder. "I'm sorry. I should know this, but what's your name?"

"Jason Stoddard."

"And you and your folks stayed out here in the rain just to thank me?"

"Yes."

"That's really something, that you'd do that. Thanks."

As the boy and his parents left, Officer Burton approached Josh. "We need to get a statement from you. Let's go inside and get out of the rain, shall we?" he said, including Josh's parents with a hand gesture.

After giving his statement to the police, and after answering a few questions for a TV news team, Josh and his parents went home.

Josh went to his room and closed the door. He went to the side of his bed and knelt down. He spoke in a whisper because his parents were nearby and once when he had been praying, his mother had opened the door to ask who he was talking to, and so now when he prayed he spoke in a whisper.

He had two things he needed to pray about—first was to give thanks that he'd been able to stop Harlan without anyone getting hurt, and the second was to ask about whether or not he should serve a mission. But as he began to pray, the tension and stress he had been through took their toll. He found it difficult to concentrate on praying. Instead, he found himself reviewing in his mind all the things that had happened. And he realized for the first time how close he had come to being killed.

After a time, he lay down on his bed and eventually fell asleep. He slept for an hour and then his father knocked on the door and told him he was wanted on the phone. "It's a TV reporter. They want to interview you for the ten o'clock news. She'd like you to come to the station at seven tonight."

For Josh, the interview was harder than the hostage situation. The woman who interviewed him kept asking him questions he had no real answer for. "Josh, how does it feel to know you might have saved some of your classmates' lives?"

"Uh . . . pretty good . . . I guess."

"We have some footage of when the police brought the suspect out."

Josh looked at the monitor where two policemen were walking Harlan out of the school. Harlan looked small, and he turned his head away from the camera as he was hustled into the backseat of a police car.

"What was going on in your mind during the ordeal?" the interviewer asked.

Josh shrugged his shoulders. "Well, I was just hoping things'd work out, that's all."

With Josh responding so briefly to her questions, the interviewer took up time describing the situation again and making Josh out to be a hero.

Later, Josh watched the interview at home with his parents. It was agonizing. He was surprised by how uncomfortable he looked and how wimpy his voice sounded. He hoped his friends weren't watching.

That night he had a hard time sleeping. He stayed up until two-thirty in the morning watching old movies and then finally fell asleep on the couch.

When he woke up the next morning, it was eleven o'clock. He could hear his mother running the vacuum cleaner in the hallway. He grabbed his quilt and dragged it back to his room and got dressed.

His mother fussed over him and even though it was almost noon, she made him pancakes and eggs. While he was eating, he picked up the morning paper. The front page had a picture of Harlan being escorted out of the school by the two police officers.

Josh glanced at the article. From the way it talked about Harlan, it might have been captioned, "Loser Messes Up Again."

Why does he wear that stupid coat all the time? Josh thought. *And his hair and that dumb half-smirk he carries around with him.*

At first Josh wasn't going to, but eventually he did read everything written about him in the paper that morning. It made him look a lot better than he was. He was going to throw the paper away, but his mother wouldn't let him. She said she wanted to keep it.

While Josh was taking a shower, he thought about what he needed to do that day. The most important thing was that he needed to decide once and for all about going on a mission. He needed to take some time to pray. Maybe if he really made an effort to ask what he should do, he'd have a strong confirmation. Not a vision necessarily, but something that would leave no doubt in his mind.

That's what I need, Josh thought. I need to know for sure what I'm supposed to do.

Josh decided to fast until after church the next day. Instead of jeans and a sweatshirt, he put on a pair of slacks and a button shirt.

And then, so he wouldn't be disturbed, he told his mother he was going to pray about whether or not he should go on a mission.

She turned off the radio, and he went to his room and closed the door. First he made his bed and cleaned up a little because he had heard once that the Spirit doesn't like messy rooms.

He knelt down. "Heavenly Father," he spoke a little louder than he usually did when he prayed because this was important and also because his mother knew what he was doing. This was an important prayer and he wanted to say it just right. But actually, there wasn't much to say. "Help me decide if I should go on a mission or not."

Nothing happened. No inspiration. No confirmation. Nothing.

Josh was disappointed. *I'm not going to give up,* he thought. *I'm going to stay here until I get an answer.*

Half an hour later, though, still nothing had happened. *This is the longest I've ever prayed,* he thought. Finally, his knees were hurting, so he got up and went to his window and looked out. It was still raining.

He wondered how Harlan was doing. He wondered if anyone had gone to see him. He regretted telling Harlan he was a loser. *I shouldn't have said that,* he thought. *He's had a hard life.* He had read about it in the newspaper. The reporters couldn't get in touch with Harlan's mother because she was out of town, indefinitely, and his step-father had as much as said he didn't care what happened to the boy.

Since not much was happening with his prayers, Josh told his mother he was going to the jail to see Harlan.

At first the woman at the desk of the county jail wasn't going to let him see Harlan, but when she recognized him as the one who had brought an end to the hostage situa-tion, she made an exception to the rule.

Josh and Harlan met on opposite sides of a thick win-dow that divided two small rooms. They spoke to each other through a phone set. Harlan was wearing a fluores-cent orange jumpsuit.

"Hello, Harlan. How's it going?"

"All right, I guess. What are you doing here?"

"Well, for one thing, I came to apologize."

"You, apologize to me? What for?"

"For saying you're a loser," Josh said.

"I am, though."

"No you're not."

"If I'm not, who is?" Harlan asked. He sounded tired, not belligerent or angry like he had in the schoolroom.

"Nobody."

"You don't really believe that, do you?"

Josh thought about Nebraska, where everyone on the

team was a winner. He shrugged his shoulders. "Well, not always, but sometimes I do."

"I don't see how you can say that about me. I can't do anything right."

At that moment Josh had the strangest feeling—as though he were a leaf floating on a river about to be swept into a whirlpool, and he could do nothing about it—a feeling that this discussion was going to end up in a place he initially had no intention of taking it.

This is how Heavenly Father is answering my prayers, he thought. *He's put me in a position to help Harlan.*

Harlan spoke into the telephone. "Did you hear what I said?"

"You said you can't do much of anything right."

"What have you got to say to that?" Harlan asked.

"Let me ask you a question first. Have you ever thought about what God is really like?"

Even before they went any further, Josh knew what he was going to do about Nebraska.

THE SWEET
SMELL OF SERVICE

"For December I think we should go caroling at the nursing home," Megan suggested at Bishop's Youth Council. Megan was the Mia Maid class president.

Cody, who represented the teachers, was intrigued by Megan, but he didn't always agree with her. "We go there every year. Why don't we do something different for a change?"

"Like what?" the bishop asked.

"I don't know."

"I know what we could do that the guys'd like," Megan said, flashing the smile she used as a weapon when she didn't agree with Cody. "We could all go in the cultural hall and shoot baskets. That'd be unique."

Cody didn't understand why people thought Megan was a nice person. She wasn't. Not at all. She had a mean streak. Why didn't anyone else see it?

"Seriously," Megan continued, "I think that at Christmastime, especially, we ought to do a service project."

"I agree," the Laurel class president said.

Cody knew he was going to lose, but he wasn't going down without a fight. "Well, if you don't like basketball, how about volleyball?"

"What have you got against going to the nursing home?" Megan asked.

"The trouble with nursing homes is they've got too many old people," Cody said.

Megan had a way of looking at people when she thought they were way off base. She was looking at him that way now. He didn't care though. Who needed her anyway? Not him, that's for sure.

Except there was that one time when he got her laughing and she couldn't stop, and the time they had danced together for almost an hour at one of the stake dances. Other than that though, he didn't care what she thought about him.

They had known each other since third grade. He had never told her so, but he thought she was the best-looking girl in school. She had a pretty, oval face and dark brown hair down to her shoulders and thick, bushy eyebrows. Just lately he had realized how much he liked to look at her face. Because they had known each other so long, it was not something he could ever admit to her. They had some classes together and he enjoyed watching her out of the corner of his eye. It was important, though, that she didn't know about it because once in a math class she had caught him staring at her. "What?" she had said.

"Nothing."

"Quit staring at me then."

"I wasn't staring at you."

"Don't lie, Cody. I know when a person is staring at me, and you were definitely staring at me."

From that he had learned to be careful.

It was on the first Tuesday in December when the whole Mutual went caroling at the Aspen Hills nursing home. As soon as they entered the building, Cody realized once again how much he didn't like the smell of old people. He tried to avoid touching any of them. They seemed like they might be infected, and he didn't want their germs on him.

Halfway down one hall they stopped to sing. Cody ended up next to Megan. She was wearing a Christmas sweater and a Santa Claus cap on her head. It would have looked dumb on anyone else, but on her it looked good.

Other girls sang like they were afraid someone might actually hear them. But not Megan. When she sang, she put her whole self into it, as though she enjoyed it.

Usually Cody didn't sing much, but being around Megan inspired him. He decided to try singing with as much enthusiasm as she had. For one song, he matched her. And she looked over at him and smiled. It was her best smile, the one he'd only seen twice before. He smiled back. It was wonderful. He wished he knew more verses to the song.

When the song ended, she said, "I'm glad you're finally starting to enjoy this after all. You remember this the next time I suggest we do a service project, okay?"

That did it for him. She had ruined everything. He hated it when girls acted like it was their whole mission in life to try to trick guys into doing the right thing.

You are so conceited, he thought. *You probably think you have a nice smile, too, don't you?*

"Let's move on down the hall," the Young Women's president called out to the group.

Cody looked around. This was supposed to be a combined activity, but all he saw were girls and a few deacons who hadn't caught on yet to the fact that guys don't sing. He knew for a fact that three guys his age had stayed behind in the cultural hall at church so they could shoot baskets. His teachers quorum adviser wasn't even singing.

There was one guy Cody's age who sang, but he didn't count because he was a music fanatic anyway.

This whole thing is for girls, Cody thought. He felt embarrassed that he'd sung so loud. He wondered what the deacons thought about him now.

As the rest of them moved on down the hall, Cody dropped back. He had had it with girls and women and dumb service projects.

It wasn't bad enough that he had to deal with this kind of thing at church. It was the same thing at home. His dad was gone a lot on business. His mother kept him busy every night doing jobs when she got home from work.

Cody decided he'd had it with caroling. If he had to jump through all of Megan's hoops to get her to like him, it wasn't worth it. If she couldn't take him the way he was, then he'd find someone who could.

But not right away. He was through with girls for now and maybe for good.

The nursing home was designed like the spokes of a wheel, with the lobby and eating area in the middle. The carolers still had several long hallways to visit.

He dropped out of the group and made his way to the TV room. Six nursing home residents were sitting in their wheelchairs in front of the TV. Three of them were slumped over, asleep. Near the back of the room there was a long, unoccupied couch. Cody sat down to watch TV. He wished he knew where the remote was because this was the same dumb documentary about sharks he saw everytime he channel-surfed at home—the one where the shark circles this big cage where a diver is hiding. Cody was so sick of seeing it, fifteen seconds at a time, that lately he had started to cheer for the shark.

An old man, leaning on a walker, came into the room.

He made his way over to the couch and eased himself down next to Cody. "Watching TV, huh?" the man asked.

Cody cautiously turned to look at the man. He was wearing a ratty old robe and a pair of frayed slippers. He needed a shave; his whiskers were white, and he smelled of Mentholatum.

Cody looked around for a place to move to but this was the only couch in the room.

"You like sharks?" the old man asked.

"Not really. I'm just waiting. I'm with a church group. We're caroling here tonight."

"I know. I heard them coming. That's why I came here."

"You came to get away from them?" Cody asked.

"Sure did. Things like that drive me crazy."

Cody smiled. The next time Megan suggested they go caroling, he'd have some ammunition.

"I've never liked to sing much," the man said.

"Me either."

"You ever have bad dreams?" the old man asked.

"Sometimes, why?"

"I have them all the time."

Cody didn't care about some old guy's bad dreams.

"I dream about the war," the old man said.

"What war?"

"The Second World War." The old man's voice was kind of shaky. "I was in the Philippines. When we were ordered to surrender, I grabbed a few supplies and slipped into the jungle during the night. I lived off what food I could find until I made contact with the underground. I fought with the underground until the island was liberated."

Cody wondered if the old man had told this story a great many times before because it sounded so much like a rehearsed speech. "That must have been really exciting."

"Too exciting. That's why I still have bad dreams."

"How can you stand to be in a place like this? You should be staying with your family."

"Don't have a family."

"How come? You never got married?"

It took the old man a long time to answer. When he replied, he seemed less rehearsed and more vulnerable. "I was married once. I got married just before I went overseas."

"What happened?"

"When I disappeared into the jungle, nobody knew where I'd gone or what I was doing. There were so many others, too, they couldn't account for. Sometimes they made mistakes. One day my wife got a telegram saying I was dead. By the time I got home two years later, she had remarried."

"She married somebody else? What did you do?" Cody asked.

"What could I do?"

"Tell the guy to move out."

"He was married to her."

"Well, so were you."

"Not in the eyes of the law."

"I'd have run him out of town."

"She was expecting a baby—his baby."

"Did she have a baby by you?"

"Yes."

"So, one each. That means you were both even."

"He'd been very good to her."

"So what! I'd have asked her to leave him. Did you ever do that?"

He shook his head. "No, we never talked. If we ever

saw each other on the street, we would always avoid each other. Finally, I realized it was no good for us to be in the same town, so I left. I went away for forty years. By the time I came back, she'd already died. That's when I started living here."

"What's your name?"

"Joe Sullivan. What's yours?"

"Cody Brown. How long were you married?"

"Two weeks, and then I had to report for duty."

"Two weeks isn't very long."

"No."

"What happened to you isn't fair," Cody stammered.

"Life isn't always fair."

"So after you got back and found out she was married, you left town. Where did you go?"

"Alaska."

"That's where I'd have gone too. I've always wanted to go there. What did you do in Alaska?"

"Got a job on an oil rig."

"There were mostly men there, right?"

"All men. At that time there were no women in jobs like that."

"That sounds real good to me," Cody said.

"You got something against women?"

"They're always after you to do something you don't want to do."

"But, usually, they're things you should do."

"Maybe so, but I don't like a woman telling me what to do."

"You'll get over that," Mr. Sullivan said.

"I don't think so."

"Maybe you'd better talk to your dad about that."

"I don't see my dad much. He's always on the road. He

sells computer software. He's gone during the week and then comes home for a day and then leaves again."

Cody saw Megan in the hall coming toward him. He got up from the couch and went to meet her.

"What are you doing?" she asked. "We need you to sing with us."

"Who told you to come get me?" Cody asked.

She blushed. "Nobody."

"Then why'd you come for me?" he asked, hoping he could get her to say she missed him.

"Because you're the only guy who sings out. Everybody else just mumbles."

"Come meet this old guy I've been talking to."

"We're supposed to be singing now," she said.

"It won't kill you to do what I want to do, once, will it? Please. It won't take very long and then I'll go sing with you."

"Who do you want me to meet?" she asked, looking around the room.

"That old man on the couch."

She glanced at Mr. Sullivan. "Why do you want me to meet him?"

That was a good question. Mr. Sullivan didn't look any better than the ones Cody usually tried to avoid whenever he came here with Church groups. He wondered why they didn't throw out that old robe of his and give him something new.

"I know he doesn't look like much, but once you get to know him . . . "

She gave him that superior smile of hers. "You're glad you came here tonight, aren't you?"

He hated it when she acted like she knew what was best for him.

"No."

"Don't give me that. You are. You're glad you met that old man. I can always tell what you're thinking, so you might as well just come out and admit that it was a really good idea for us to come here."

"I never said it was a bad idea. All I said was I thought we should do something else for a change. Are you going to meet this old geezer or not?"

"All right, but we're supposed to be singing now."

"Oh, yeah? Well, listen—the main reason he's out here is he can't stand carolers."

"You're making that up."

"I am not. If you don't believe me, ask him. He'll tell you. If *you* lived here, would *you* want people coming around and singing their heads off when you're trying to rest? I wouldn't, that's for sure. Come meet him and let him tell you about himself." He took a big risk and grabbed Megan's hand and led her to where Mr. Sullivan was sitting. "Mr. Sullivan, this is my friend Megan."

Mr. Sullivan stared at Megan as though he'd just seen a ghost. He mumbled something. Cody let go of Megan's hand and bent down so he could hear better. "What did you say?"

"Is this Rita?" he whispered softly so Megan couldn't hear.

"No, this is Megan."

It was as if Mr. Sullivan had gone away to a different time. He looked confused at first but then he nodded his head. "Yes, of course. It couldn't be Rita. Rita's dead."

Cody stood back up.

"What did he say?" Megan asked.

Cody was embarrassed for Mr. Sullivan that he couldn't keep things straight. "Nothing much."

Mr. Sullivan reached for Megan's hand and held it until she pulled away.

"I don't like the way he's looking at me," she said softly to Cody.

"I think maybe he's just a little confused right now."

Mr. Sullivan rubbed his scruffy whiskers. "You look like someone I used to know when I was your age. She was a beautiful woman, just like you'll be someday."

Megan looked embarrassed, but she said, "Thank you."

"Mr. Sullivan, tell Megan the story you were telling me."

"What story is that?" Mr. Sullivan asked.

"You know, about how you got married during the Second World War."

Mr. Sullivan looked away and mumbled, "Married? No, I was never married."

"Yes you were, remember? Just before they made you go back to the war. But the island you were on got captured so you had to hide in the jungle for a long time. But your wife didn't know that. She thought you were dead, and she married someone else. Then when you came home and found her married to someone else, you couldn't stand it, so you went off to Alaska for a long time. Do you remember all that now?"

Mr. Sullivan stared blankly into space.

"I guess he's not feeling very well," Cody said to Megan.

"That's okay. We can talk to him some other time. Right now we need to get back and sing some more," she said softly to Cody. She reached out to let him hold her hand. That was good, except it was the same hand Mr. Sullivan had held. Cody thought about all the germs that might have transferred onto her hand, but it was the only hand she was offering, so he took it.

"You like him, don't you?" she asked.

"Not really."

"I think you do."

"Maybe, just a little."

"You don't fool me, Cody, not one bit, so don't think you do."

They walked down the hall holding hands, but just before they caught up with their group, she pulled away so nobody would see. He understood. Kids would make a big deal out of it and make fun of them. But he hoped she'd let him hold her hand in the car on the way home, where it'd be dark and nobody would notice.

His great plans were ruined though. After they finished caroling, somehow, in the confusion, Cody and Megan ended up in different cars. And whoever was driving the car Megan was riding in dropped her off on the way to the church, so he didn't get a chance to see her anymore that night.

When he got home, his father was home from a road trip. They talked for about half an hour and then his father told Cody to get to bed.

"Do you ever wish you weren't gone so much?" Cody asked.

"All the time."

"Me too. Well, goodnight."

Cody couldn't sleep. Finally, at eleven-thirty, he got up and went into the kitchen. His dad was sitting at the kitchen table, working on his laptop.

"What happened in the Philippines?" Cody asked.

"When?"

"During the Second World War."

"I wasn't there."

"I need to know."

"Why?"

"For a class," Cody lied. He wasn't sure why.

"Why don't you look it up in the encyclopedia?" his dad suggested.

Cody nodded his head and went to the bookshelf where they kept the encyclopedia. It had been there ever since he could remember. Nobody used it anymore, though.

He read about the war in the Pacific. There *was* some fighting in the Philippines. Maybe it happened just like Mr. Sullivan had said. He could have slipped into the jungle and disappeared.

He must have felt so alone to be out there in the jungle all by himself, especially when every step could get him killed, Cody thought. *He's alone now, too.*

Cody said goodnight to his dad and went back to bed. Lying there in the darkness, he kept thinking about Mr. Sullivan. *Maybe he's always been alone. And when he dies, nobody will care. What does it matter that he looks so awful in that robe and those slippers and that he never shaves and that he smells like an old person? It's what he is that counts, not the way he looks. Maybe I could get him a robe for Christmas and some new slippers, and then he'd look better.* Cody stayed awake for a long time before finally falling asleep.

The next thing he knew it was morning and his mother was in his room, opening up the window shades. "Cody, it's time to get up."

"There's no school today. We're on vacation."

"I know, but you can't lie around sleeping all day. I made a list of jobs I need you to do. Get them done first thing and then you'll have the rest of the day for whatever you want."

"Is Dad here?"

"No, he had to go out again. He'll be gone a couple of days."

"I wish he didn't have to be gone so much."

"I know. So do I. But these are hard times. He's lucky to have a job. Oh, I'm leaving some money on the table for you to buy a Christmas present for your dad."

Cody slept until ten-thirty, got dressed, and then quickly did the jobs on his list. At eleven he called Megan. Her mother answered.

"Is Megan there?" Cody asked.

"Just a minute."

Megan answered.

"What are you doing?" Cody asked. "I want you to come with me to get Mr. Sullivan a Christmas present and then we can take it to him."

"Why don't you do it by yourself? My mom has a whole bunch of things she wants me to do."

"No, I want you to come with me."

"Well . . . I'll ask. Hold on, okay?"

"Tell your mom it's a service project."

There was a long wait before Megan came on the phone again.

"She says it will be okay because it's a service project, but for it not to take all day."

"Ask her if she can drive us to the mall and wait for us to get something for him and then drop us off at the nursing home."

"I'll ask, but I'm not sure she'll do it because she's really busy."

A short time later, Megan returned to the phone. "She says she's too busy to run us all over town. And she can only spare me for an hour."

Cody's hopes sank. It would take a couple of hours walking to go to the mall and back to the nursing home and then back to Megan's place again. "We'll need more than an hour."

"Maybe you'd better go without me then," she said.

"All right, but could you do me a favor?"

"What?"

"I need to know the first names of your grandmothers and great-grandmothers. Ask your mom if you don't know."

"Cody, my mom's in a bad enough mood as it is. Don't make it worse."

"Please, just ask her."

"All right, but don't say I didn't warn you."

A short time later Megan's mother got on the phone. "Why do you need to know?"

"Because . . . because I'm making a Christmas present for Megan and I need to know all that stuff."

"What kind of a present?"

Cody was making this all up as he went along. "I guess you could say it's kind of a family history present."

"Just a minute. I'll get our group sheets."

It took Megan's mother several minutes before she returned. She told Cody the first names of Megan's grand-mothers. There were no Ritas. And then she started reading from the group sheets. The first great-grandmother she read was a Rita.

"Stop. That's it. How many times was Rita married?" Cody asked.

"Just once."

It could still work if Rita had hidden from her children the fact that she had been married during the war. "Can you tell me this—Was her first child born before she was married?"

That was the wrong thing to say. Megan's mom wasn't very patient anyway, and now she sounded mad. "My gosh, Cody. Why would you even think such a thing?"

"Just look at the date, okay?"

There was a long pause and then a formal reply. "Everything is in order, the way it should be."

Cody wondered if Megan's mom had seen there was a

problem but wasn't going to tell him. He decided not to press it any further. "Did your grandmother ever talk about the Second World War to you?"

"No. Cody, look . . .."

"I know. All right, thanks. Can I talk to Megan again?"

"She's real busy right now. Call her back after she's finished her jobs. Oh, and by the way, I'll be *very interested* to see that family history Christmas present you're making for Megan."

"Me too," Cody said weakly.

A few minutes later he left the house on foot, headed for the mall. He had the money his mother had given him for his dad's present. He was planning on spending only a small part on a present for Mr. Sullivan but that was before he found out how expensive robes were. Even at the discount stores, it cost most of what his mother had given him, but he went ahead and bought the robe anyway. Then, on his way out of the store, he saw a display for Old Spice aftershave. It was the brand his grandfather always wore. Cody thought Mr. Sullivan might like it too. And so he bought a bottle.

On the walk to the nursing home, he wondered what he was going to give his dad for Christmas. He'd spent nearly all the money his mother had given him. *Maybe a family history gift,* he thought, *as soon as I figure out how I'm going to do that for Megan.*

When he got to the nursing home, he went to the main desk. "I need to see Mr. Sullivan," he said.

"He's probably walking the halls. That's what he does every day about this time," the attendant said.

A few minutes later Cody found Mr. Sullivan. He was using a walker to support himself as he walked. "Cody, hello. How are you? Think you can keep up with me?"

Cody smiled and walked beside Mr. Sullivan. "I

brought you a present." Mr. Sullivan stopped. Cody showed him the two gift-wrapped packages.

"My gosh, would you look at that!"

"The store wrapped them for me. You can open them now if you want."

"No, I'd like to wait, so I'll have something to open for Christmas."

"You might want to shave before you use them," Cody hinted.

"I'll surely do that. Thank you so much."

A nurse walking by offered to take the presents to Mr. Sullivan's room. He thanked her and gave her the packages.

They started down the hall together. When he walked, Mr. Sullivan kept his head down, his eyes focused a few feet ahead of him.

"The people who work here like you, don't they?" Cody asked.

"I guess so. They're very good to us."

"What did you think of the girl I introduced you to last night?"

"She's very nice."

"Can I ask you a question? Was your wife's name Rita?"

He stopped walking and glanced over at Cody. "Yes."

"When you saw that girl last night, did she remind you of Rita?"

"Yes, she did."

"Guess what? One of that girl's great-grandmothers was named Rita."

"I wondered if that might be the case."

"Is that why you didn't tell her about Rita?" Cody asked.

Mr. Sullivan nodded his head. "Rita didn't want her

children to know she had been married before. I've tried to honor her wishes. And you must promise not to tell that girl . . . "

"Megan."

"Yes."

"I won't tell her."

"Thank you."

They walked a few more feet. "If you want me to, I could bring her by sometime, though."

Mr. Sullivan stopped walking. He leaned on his walker and closed his eyes. Cody wondered if, in his mind, he had gone back to the two weeks he had been married to Rita.

"Are you okay, Mr. Sullivan?"

The old man lifted his head and stood up a little straighter, like an old but still proud lion. "I am fine, thank you."

"You want me to bring her by sometime?"

"Do you think she'd come to see me?"

Cody smiled. "I think so. She's very big on service projects."

"Your coming to see me today—was that a service project?"

Cody thought about it. "No, not really. This is different. It's more like coming to see a friend."

"I'm honored to be your friend. Walk back to my room with me, will you? You gave me presents, so I want to give you one."

"You don't have to do that."

"Oh, but I do. That's what friends do."

Mr. Sullivan's room was the last room on the right, at the end of the hall. Cody noticed a man lying in the other bed.

"Jacob, this is my friend Cody. He's come to visit us today."

The man in the other bed looked off into space.

"Jacob is having a hard time right now," Mr. Sullivan said.

He went to a drawer and pulled out a medal and placed it in Cody's hand. "I want you to have this."

Cody looked down at the medal. It was heavy, made out of bronze, and it was threaded on a faded ribbon. "What is this?" Cody asked.

"Just a medal."

"Is it from the War?"

"Yes."

"I can't take it."

"Why not?"

"This must be very important to you."

"I've got more. I won't miss this one."

"No, I can't take it. It wouldn't be right."

Mr. Sullivan placed his withered hand on Cody's shoulder. "They'll just throw them all away when I die, anyway, so you might as well have it."

"Why me?"

He reached over and closed Cody's fingers around the medal. "Just take it."

Cody nodded his head. "All right. It will be my best present. Thanks a lot." It was awkward for Cody, not knowing if he should hug Mr. Sullivan or if they should just shake hands. He did neither. "Well, I'd better be going."

"Yes, of course. Thank you for coming."

"I'll come back as soon as I can. And I'll bring Megan with me. Oh, it might be a while because we're going away for Christmas."

"Whenever you come, it will be fine. I'll be here."

"Well, good-bye. And thanks for the medal."

As he walked down the hall, Cody looped the ribbon

around his neck and tucked the medal under his shirt so it wouldn't be noticeable.

He felt better than he'd felt in a long time. So good in fact that when he came to a woman in a wheelchair, he wished her a Merry Christmas.

The woman, who had been slumped over a bit, staring at the floor, looked up at him. "Are you one of my grandsons?" she asked with a smile.

"No, but if you want me to be your grandson, just for today, I'd like that."

They clasped hands, and she pulled his hand up and pressed it to her cheek. "Good-bye, now, dear," she said. Backing away, Cody waved and then continued on down the hall.

As he made his way out the main entrance of Aspen Hills nursing home, he didn't see old people. He only saw new friends.

JAMIE'S FIRST STAND

Jamie liked to do her homework on the kitchen table after supper because it was warmer there than in her room and because there was always something to snack on if she got hungry. Usually she put on earphones and listened to music while she worked, but that night, when her mother called Jamie's aunt on the phone, Jamie kept the earphones on and turned the music off, so she could listen in without her mother knowing.

Jamie knew they would be talking about her because, for the first time in her life, Jamie was in trouble.

" . . . The damage had already been done by the time we had any clue what was happening," her mother said into the phone. "Looking back on it now, I can see how foolish we were. I mean, it's not like we weren't warned. We should have listened to the people who told us not to let our children have any contact with them."

There was a pause and then, in answer to a question, her mother said, "Right next door! They have a daughter Jamie's age named Heather. They moved here last year. Jamie and Heather were both in girls' choir and had some of the same classes, and they both went out for soccer this year. She seemed like such a nice girl, too. But, of course, that's what they want you to believe. Well, before we knew it, Jamie and Heather were good friends, doing everything together. Her parents even had us over once for dessert. They seemed like nice people, even then."

Another pause and then her mother continued. "Well, yes, I know that now, but I didn't know it then. I must confess we really had no idea what was going on. About a month ago Jamie spent the night at their home. That's when it must have begun. When she came home, she apparently had a copy of their Bible." Another pause. "No, of course I didn't know she had it. If I'd known, I would have made her take it back. Since then, she's been reading it behind our backs in her room at night. Last night she told us she wants to become a Mormon. Well, of course we said no."

Staring blankly at her algebra book, Jamie remembered how frustrating it had been when she told her parents she wanted to be baptized. They would't even listen to her.

Her mother continued on the phone. "The problem is she still wants to become a Mormon. John said that if she still wants to join when she turns eighteen, she can do it, but it will mean she won't get any support from us for college. . . . What did she say? She said it doesn't matter what we do because she is going to join their church as soon as she turns eighteen. I don't know what they did to her, but we can't talk her out of it. I don't know what to do. Now she's talking about becoming a Mormon after she graduates from high school and then moving to Utah to work. John told her he'd disown her if she did that, but she said it didn't matter, she has to do what she knows to be right. . . . No, I haven't talked to Heather's parents. I don't want to have any more contact with anyone in the family. . . . I hate to ask this, but is there any chance David could come down and try to talk some sense into her? David is her favorite uncle. It's a long way, and I know how busy he is, but if he can just come down and talk to her, maybe he can help her get rid of these foolish ideas. At least he has the education to know exactly where she's been led wrong. . . . Yes, anytime. Oh, thank you so much. Tell him it will be an answer to our prayers."

Jamie resented being treated like a child. Her parents wouldn't even listen to her. And now they were bringing in their big gun—Uncle David, her mother's brother, an ordained minister. In all the family gatherings, she couldn't remember him ever losing an argument. It didn't matter what it was about—cars, politics, or religion.

Not only that, but for as long as she could remember, she and her uncle David had always had a special affection for one another. At first it was probably because they both liked ice cream so much. When the two families were together, he used to take her out, even past her bedtime, just the two of them, for double-dipped cones.

Uncle David had two sons but no daughters. Jamie was his only niece. He called her a rose among thorns. She always liked being called a rose.

When she was very little and he would read *Goldilocks and the Three Bears* to her as a bedtime story, she was impressed by his rich baritone voice. When he was Papa Bear, it seemed to shake the room.

In the third grade she discovered jumping rope. She would tie one end of the rope to the garage door and then go off in search of someone to turn the other end. Once at a family reunion, by the end of the first day she couldn't find anyone else willing to stand in the driveway and turn the rope for her, but her uncle David could never say no to her. He stood out in the hot sun, while she jumped, singing in rhythm to the slapping of the rope against the driveway. By late afternoon, after being in the sun so long, his face and nearly bald head were badly sunburned. While giving his sermon the next day, he joked about it to his congregation and had Jamie stand so they would know who'd kept him in the blazing sun for so long.

Uncle David had a wonderful speaking voice. From the pulpit, when he quoted an Old Testament prophet, he could shake the church's foundations. Unfortunately, though, he couldn't carry a tune. Jamie didn't mind though. It all sounded fine to her because he was her favorite uncle and because she knew he loved her.

About the time she was in seventh grade, they began to share their love of words, of phrases neatly turned, of sentences with double meanings and word puzzles. They loved to stump each other with a puzzle or a riddle and for a time, while Jamie was in junior high, the two of them had exchanged riddles in the mail.

She had always known her uncle was a man of God. How could anyone doubt it? He loved people and his ministry. All he had ever wanted was to do what God wanted him to do. She loved him for that. She had always wanted to be like him. She had always wanted him to be proud of her.

And now she was going against what he believed. She had heard him say negative things about the Mormons. That was in her mind whenever she read the Book of Mormon, but she never found the bad things he said were in it. When she finally realized she wanted to be baptized, she hoped she could avoid talking to him about her decision. It would be so much easier that way.

But that wasn't going to be. She would have to talk to him. She knew he would be disappointed in her. She hoped it would not mean the end of the fun relationship they had always enjoyed with each other.

Her mother hung up the phone and glanced over at her. "Jamie? Jamie, turn off your music please. I have something to say."

Jamie pretended to turn the volume down and removed her earphones.

"Your Uncle David is going to make a special trip just to talk to you. When he comes here, I want you to listen carefully to what he has to say."

"It won't make any difference."

"How can you do this to us after all we've done for you?" her mother demanded.

"I'm not doing anything to you. I've found something better, that's all. Why do you have to take everything so personal?"

"It's that book, isn't it? Well, I'll put a stop to this once and for all."

Her mother stormed out of the room, and Jamie could hear her in Jamie's room moving things, opening drawers, and then slamming them shut again. A short time later she returned. "Where have you hidden it? I want you to go get that book and give it to me. I will not have it in my home."

"You have no right to go into my room and go through my things," Jamie said.

"I have a right to do anything I want in this house! And if you don't tell me where it is, I'll tear your room apart until I find it!"

"I don't go through your things."

"Listen to me! You can't stay in this house anymore unless you give me that book." Her mother sounded nearly hysterical.

"Are you throwing me out of the house?" Jamie asked.

"Yes, get out, go live with the Mormons! That's what you really want, isn't it?"

"No, I want to stay here."

"You can't stay here the way you are now so just get out! I want you packed and out of here in thirty minutes! I mean it, Jamie. Thirty minutes!"

Not believing what she was hearing, Jamie slowly stood up.

Her mother seemed out of control. "Get going! If you plan to take anything with you when you leave, you'd better start packing because when the thirty minutes is up, I'm throwing you out of this house. I mean it, Jamie."

With tears streaming down her face, Jamie stumbled up the stairs to her room. She went to her closet and stared at all her clothes. She grabbed her favorite Sunday dress and held it close to her and sobbed and then slowly collapsed in a heap on the floor. Something was dreadfully wrong. Religion shouldn't make people act like this.

"You have twenty-five minutes!" her mother practically screamed from the bottom of the stairs.

Jamie wiped her eyes and went to the garage to get the luggage set she'd been given on her last birthday. She dragged the bags to her room and started shoving clothes into the suitcase. She soon realized she was going to need more room, so she went to the garage and got some large leaf bags and returned to her room and continued packing. While she packed, she could hear her mother in the master bedroom, sobbing.

She went to the kitchen to use the phone. She called the Baxters next door. Heather answered the phone.

She closed her eyes and fought back the tears. "Heather, my mom is throwing me out of the house."

"Why?"

"Because I wouldn't give her my Book of Mormon."

"What are you going to do?" Heather asked.

"Can I come stay with you?"

"You know you can."

"I've got just a few more minutes before she says I have to be out of the house, so I'm just going to dump all my things on the sidewalk. When I get everything out, can you help me carry them over to your house?"

"Sure, whatever you want. My mom's not home, but I'm sure it'll be okay for you to stay with us."

Jamie returned to her room. Because it had been her room since the third grade, it was full of memories. She stood in front of her bookshelf and tried to decide what books to take. Her parents believed so much in the value of reading, they had showered books on her from the time she was a little girl. She realized that it was partly because she liked to read so much that she'd been able to get through so much of the Book of Mormon in such a short time.

She had hidden her copy of the Book of Mormon in the bookshelf behind a history book her dad had given her for her last birthday. She found it and put it in one of her suitcases.

When she was about to start high school, her parents had given her a computer and a printer. She loved using it but realized she'd have to leave it behind because even if she took it she'd never be able to figure out how to attach all the cables. Her father had done that for her when they first got it.

She stood in her room and tried to sort out her thoughts. *Why is this happening?* she wondered. *I don't want to leave.*

She grabbed a lawn bag and went into the bathroom and began dropping her cosmetics into it. She used to have braces and still needed to wear a retainer at night, so she dropped that in the plastic bag, too.

She opened the garage door and pushed her mountain bike out into the driveway. She couldn't bear to leave that behind.

As she started back inside, she saw her mother

standing at the window of the master bedroom watching her. *Maybe she won't let me take the bike,* she thought.

Jamie went inside and did a quick walk-through of the house.

There was still so much she wouldn't be able to take with her. She stopped at a bookshelf and picked up the family scrapbook. They'd kept a scrapbook of every vacation the family had ever taken. She thumbed through it. There was a picture of her wearing a swimsuit—a scrawny ten-year-old on a beach in California standing alongside her parents.

They've been good to me, she thought. She put the scrapbook back on the bookshelf and returned to her room. She started hauling everything out to the sidewalk. *It's a public sidewalk,* she thought. *She can't yell at me for leaving my things there.*

When Jamie came back into the house, her mother was standing in the hallway. "I've changed my mind. I don't want you to go," she said through her tears.

"I don't want to go, either, Mom."

"Stay then."

"What about the book?" Jamie asked.

"Does it really mean so much to you?"

"Yes, it does. It means very much to me."

"All right, you can have the book in your room, but don't let me ever see it because if I do, I'll burn it."

"All right."

Her mother turned to go back into her room.

"Mom?"

"What?"

"I love you."

They ran to each other and threw their arms around each other and held on.

*   *   *

Jamie kept her things packed because she didn't know what would come of her uncle's visit. She was afraid that if she continued to stand up for what she believed, even after her uncle had done what he could to talk her out of it, she still might be thrown out of the house.

Uncle David arrived Friday at six-thirty. He had driven two hundred miles to get there. As soon as he arrived, he told Jamie's mother he couldn't stay overnight. He had to get back home for a Saturday activity sponsored by his church.

When Jamie first saw him, she wasn't sure what to expect, but he greeted her with the same enthusiasm he had always shown for her.

She hadn't seen him for more than a year. He looked thinner and older than Jamie remembered him. He didn't seem like the same man, with a booming voice and a love for ice cream and songs badly sung, the man she remembered from when she was little. She imagined it was because he was disappointed in her, but then she remembered he had recently experienced his own personal tragedies. Last year his oldest son, Robert, had been seriously injured in an auto accident. He was only now able to walk slowly, with the aid of a walker.

Jamie knew she was no match for her uncle in a religious debate. He was an ordained minister who had spent his entire professional life studying the Bible and preaching the gospel. Not only that, but in college he had been on the debate team. She had once heard him say that if he hadn't gone into the ministry, he would have become a trial lawyer.

It was hard for her to imagine they would ever disagree on anything. So many of the lessons she had received about Christianity she had learned from him. He didn't just talk religion, he lived it every day. He visited jails and nursing homes and cared for the homeless. He worked with gang members in a midnight basketball program. He once headed up a drive to raise money for a shelter for battered women.

There was very little about Uncle David she would ever be able to find fault with. In their family, he was the best example of what it meant to be a Christian.

She did not look forward to their discussion. She realized she knew little about what Mormons believed. She hadn't taken the missionary lessons. She had not even read the Book of Mormon all the way through. She had read four hundred pages. What could she say to defend herself against someone who had gone to college for four years and then to divinity school to become a minister?

After supper, her uncle asked if he could talk to her. She nodded her head, went upstairs, said a quick prayer, retrieved her copy of the Book of Mormon, and brought it downstairs to the kitchen.

Her parents left them alone to talk, saying they needed to do some grocery shopping.

Jamie and Uncle David sat in the kitchen on opposite sides of the table. He had five books he'd brought with him, the Bible plus four other thick volumes. All Jamie had was her paperback copy of the Book of Mormon.

Uncle David was used to taking charge in any situation. "First of all, Jamie, I want you to know that I have a great deal of respect for Mormons. They've always been strong on the importance of families. Not only that, but all the Mormons I've ever known were honest people and hard workers. Also, their church teaches its members not to smoke or drink or use drugs. All of that is very good. I have nothing but respect for the way they live their lives."

Jamie nodded weakly and braced for the inevitable.

"But the simple truth is that, as good a people as they are, they're not Christian."

"They say they're Christian."

He smiled at her naivety. "I could say I was a giraffe, too, but would that make me one?"

"No. But if you were a giraffe, even if I said you weren't, you'd still be one."

They were back to word games again. He suppressed a smile. She knew if they weren't talking about such serious things, he would have complimented her on her quick comeback.

"The point is that it doesn't matter what they *say* they are. What matters is what they believe. They're not Christian, Jamie. They're a cult. I'm sorry you got mixed up with them." He picked up one of his books. "Here, let me read what someone else has written."

He read several passages he'd marked in the book. The more he read, the worse she felt. He just kept coming at her with quotes from books. She knew there was no stopping him. She had no arguments to use against what he was reading. It would take months of research to find out the truth behind each accusation.

Maybe he's right, she thought. *Maybe I have been deceived.* She tried to get back the feeling she'd had when she read the Book of Mormon, but with him tearing apart the character of Joseph Smith, she felt like she had been caught in an avalanche.

"Excuse me, I have to go to the bathroom," she finally said as an excuse to escape.

"All right, I'll wait."

She went into the bathroom and closed the door. She looked at herself in the mirror. Her face was flushed, and she felt like she was going to be sick. How could she stand up to her uncle? It was not only what he said. It was the way he said it. So positive, so self-assured. Not only that, but she knew he loved her. And he loved Jesus. How could he be wrong and she be right? It didn't make sense.

She knelt on the floor and placed her folded arms on the side of the bathtub and rested her head on her arms. "Oh, God, please help me. If what Heather's told me is true, help me to know what to say." She said the words softly because she didn't want her uncle to hear her.

She closed her prayer and opened her eyes. She grabbed a towel and sat on it because the tile was cold. She sat cross-legged and looked around the room. From that height the room looked strange, the angles somehow distorted and unfamiliar. *This is what it's like to be little,* she thought.

In her mind she saw herself once again as a little girl, in the summer out in the driveway, jumping rope as her uncle chanted out in rhythm to the slapping of the rope, "Peas porridge hot, peas porridge cold, peas porridge in the pot, nine days old."

"Again, Uncle David," she would say.

"Peas porridge hot, peas porridge cold, peas porridge in the pot, nine days old."

"Again, Uncle David."

This doesn't make any sense, she thought, *that he, with all his education, with a lifetime of wanting only to do what God wanted him to do, should be wrong and I be right.*

Why not just trust him, she thought. *What would be so wrong with that? That's what I'll do,* she decided. *It's the only reasonable thing to do. I love him. I've always loved him.*

She stood up and looked in the mirror. Her face was a mess, especially her puffy eyes. *Uncle David will start calling me a thorn among roses if I don't do something,* she thought with a smile.

She did the best she could do to fix herself up. As she put her hand on the doorknob to leave the bathroom, one single powerful thought came into her mind. *What if it really is true and the only way Uncle David or my mom and dad can know it is through me? What if I'm the only link they'll have in this life?*

Thoughts began racing into her mind. It wasn't whether she loved her uncle or not. It was whether what she'd read was true or not. *That* was the question that had to be answered.

But how can I do anything against him? she thought.

Almost immediately, she answered her own question. *He doesn't know anything about the Book of Mormon,* she thought.

As she reflected back over all he'd said against the Mormon Church, very little of it had anything to do with the Book of Mormon. He had ignored the one book she had read. She felt a calmness come over her. It was the answer to her prayer. She must focus everything she said on that book.

She returned to the kitchen. Her uncle was ready to begin again.

She picked up the Book of Mormon and pointed to the cover. "It says here that this book is Another Witness of Jesus Christ."

"They can say that, but the truth is they don't believe the things that Jesus taught."

"Like what?"

"They don't believe in the grace of Jesus Christ. Maybe that's why they work so hard."

"Have you ever read this?" she asked.

Her uncle glanced disparagingly at the book. "I've read parts of it."

"Why didn't you read all of it?"

"I read enough to know that it isn't true."

"What did you read that wasn't true?"

He shrugged his shoulders. "It's been a long time since I read it."

"How many pages did you read?" she asked.

"I can't remember."

"Well, was it five pages or a hundred pages or three hundred pages?"

"More like five pages."

"What made you read the five pages?" Jamie asked.

"It was part of a course I took at divinity school."

"What was the name of the course?"

"What difference does it make?"

"Just curious, that's all."

"Well, if you must know, we were studying cults."

"So you really didn't go into it with an open mind, did you?"

Her uncle leaned forward. "They are a cult, Jamie, by every definition you can think of. That's why your parents are so concerned. That's why your mom asked me to come here."

"I just want to know how you could decide this book isn't true when you only read five pages."

"Why can't you just take my word? I'm your uncle. I love you."

"I know you do. I love you too."

"If you were as old as me, if you had the education I have, you'd know, like I do, that the Mormons are way off the mark."

"If it's so obvious they're wrong, prove it from this book. If you can prove Mormons aren't Christian from this book, then do it. If you can't, then I think we're both wasting our time."

"I haven't read all of it."   .

She smiled. "That's not my fault, is it?" She turned to the end of the book. "Look, it's five hundred and thirty-one pages long. If it's so obviously wrong, like you say it is, I bet we could turn to just about any page and find a big mistake." She tried to hand him the book but he refused to take it.

"The trouble with Mormons is they believe in Joseph Smith more than they do in Jesus Christ," her uncle said.

"Is that in here?" she asked.

"Put the book away and listen to me," her uncle complained. "Why won't you accept my word? Have you graduated from college? Have you been to divinity school? Have you worked all your life as a disciple of Christ? When I tell you they're not Christian, you should listen to me. They don't believe in Jesus Christ."

"Show me where it says that in here," she said, picking up the book again. "Look, how about if we do this. I'll look in the index and find where it talks about Jesus Christ, and I'll read each entry, and you tell me what's wrong with what it says."

He grabbed the book and slammed it down on the table. "Listen to me! They used to have more than one wife. Is that what you'd expect from a Christian religion?"

"So . . . you really don't want to talk about the book, do you?"

"No."

"Why not?"

"Because there are too many other things to talk about."

"Things you were told when you were taking that course about cults in divinity school? Do you really think that was a fair hearing of what they believe, especially when you've never read more than five pages of the book?"

"I don't have to read the book to know they're wrong."

"I've read most of it. What I've read I've believed. Do you want me to read the parts to you that I really liked?"

"No."

"We don't really have much to talk about then, do we?"

"I can see you have a closed mind about this."

"And you don't?" she asked.

"Jamie, listen to me. I'm your uncle, and I love you like you were my own daughter. Do you know how much you're going to hurt your parents if you go ahead with this?"

"I know they're not very happy with me now. But what would you do if you were me? What would you do if you discovered something that is wonderful. Would you walk away from it?"

He ignored the question. "What will you do if your mom and dad disown you?"

Her shoulders slumped. "I don't know. Do the best I can, I guess."

"That's easy to say now, but you don't know what it means to be totally on your own. Maybe I shouldn't say this, but it's true—you've been spoiled your whole life. You've been given everything. You don't know what it's like to be totally on your own. Believe me, it's no picnic."

"I know that. I don't know what I'll do if they kick me out. But what else can I do? This is what you'd do if you were me."

"Me? Don't bring me into this to try to justify your actions."

"But it's true. If you'd read what I've read when you were my age, you'd be doing the same thing. Because to you truth is more important than anything. I think I might have inherited that from you."

His warm smile broke the tension. "You can't inherit something from an uncle."

"I did. I got my love of ice cream from you, didn't I?"

He laughed in spite of the agitation he was feeling and reached across the table to hold her hand. "What are we ever going to do with you?"

"I don't know. Just trust me. That's about all you can do. I'm no dummy, you know."

"I know."

She found what she was looking for in the index. "Okay, here it is. Under the topic Jesus Christ—I'll read some of these, and you tell me when I come to one that's dead wrong. That should be really easy for you. Okay?"

Her uncle sighed. "Okay."

She started reading: "*Messiah to be baptized by John in Bethabara; Messiah's name to be Jesus Christ; look forward with steadfastness unto Christ; we talk of Christ, we rejoice in Christ, we preach of Christ, we prophesy of Christ; . . . can we follow Jesus save we are willing to keep Father's commandments; feast upon words of Christ, for they tell you all ye should do; . . . I glory in my Jesus.*" She stopped. "Did you find a mistake in any of that?"

"No," he said.

"Okay, how about this? This part talks about the atonement of Jesus Christ. *Son to be lifted up upon cross and slain for sins of world; Messiah offers himself a sacrifice for sin, to answer ends of law; . . . atonement must be infinite; atonement satisfies demands of justice; God raises man from everlasting death by power of atonement; . . . be reconciled unto God through atonement of Christ; if no atonement, all mankind must be lost.*"

"Stop," he said.

"Did you find a mistake?" she asked.

"No."

"Do you want to read the book yourself? Because if you do, I can get you a copy, too."

"No."

"What then?"

"Mormons don't believe that it is only through the grace of Jesus Christ that a person can be saved."

"Really? Let me look it up." She started turning pages. "Okay, here it is . . . grace . . . I'll just read through them to see what I can find. . . . *only in and through grace of God that men are saved; my soul delighteth in the Lord's grace; by grace we are saved, after all we can do; the Lord showeth us our weakness that we may know it is by his grace that we have power.*"

"That's enough," her uncle said.

"Was that last one wrong?"

"No," her uncle said softly.

"It's the way it makes you feel, isn't it? The same thing happens to me when I read it. That's how I know it's true."

"It can't be true. Nothing you can say will convince me otherwise."

"I guess we're a lot alike then, aren't we?" she asked. "I can't convince you, and you can't convince me."

He nodded his head. "You know what? We're both too stubborn for our own good."

"That's why you've always been my favorite uncle."

"Don't try to sweet-talk me."

"I'm not."

They both knew it was over.

He put his elbows on the table, placed his forefingers together and touched his lips a few times as he went over their discussion in his mind. Then he looked up at her and smiled. "You did a good job defending your position."

"Wonder where I got that from?" she said with a smile.

He looked over at her and swept back a few strands of hair from her face. "I think I've created a monster."

"Probably."

He sighed. "I shouldn't even bring this up after the

way you've behaved, but I did bring us some ice cream. It's in the freezer. Want some?"

"You know the answer to that question." She gave him a warm smile.

They ate ice cream and talked about the good times.

By the time her parents returned, the ice cream was gone. Her uncle asked if he could talk with her parents alone. Jamie went upstairs to await the verdict.

She knew they were discussing her fate. Now she felt that her uncle was on her side.

It began to snow. She stood at the window and watched it flutter down. When she saw her uncle walking out to his car, she ran down the stairs and outside and into his arms. She thanked him for coming and told him she loved him. With tears in his eyes, he smiled, and told her he loved her too.

When she returned to the house, her parents were waiting for her.

"I don't know what you said to Uncle David, but he's not as concerned about you as he was when he first got here," her mother said.

"Do you want to know what he said just before he left?" her father asked.

"What?"

"That we should be very proud of raising a daughter like you who stands up for what she believes. That's why we've decided we're not going to throw you out into the cold," her father said with a slight smile. "We want you to stay."

"Can I keep the book?" Jamie asked.

"Yes," her father said, "but we're not going to give you permission to be baptized until you turn eighteen. We do have that power you know."

"Can I go to church with Heather?" Jamie asked.

"Yes, but at least once a month we want you to go to church with us," her mother said.

Jamie nodded her head. It was a reasonable request. "All right. Can I take the missionary discussions?"

Almost simultaneously her father said yes and her mother said no. "I don't like the idea of you being brain-washed," her mother explained.

"If you want, they could give the lessons to all of us at the same time," Jamie said.

Again, her father said yes, but her mother said no.

"We'll discuss it and let you know," her father said.

"Mom and Dad?"

"Yes."

"You both taught me to never be afraid of standing up for what I believe in."

Her mother smiled through her tears. "Maybe that wasn't such a good idea after all."

"It was. This is all going to work out for the best, you'll see."

"I wish I believed that."

Jamie excused herself and went to her room and knelt down by her bed and thanked God for answering her prayers.

Nothing more was said about it until the next day. Jamie had stayed up late to help her mother bake cookies and then do dishes. As they stood side by side near the sink facing out into the stormy night, her mother said, "Do Mormons believe in Christmas?"

"They do, Mom."

"Well, at least that's the same."

When the last dish was dried, Jamie started up to her room.

"Jamie, are you sure you know what you're doing?"

"I do, Mom. It's the best thing for me."

"I think you're doing the wrong thing, but I do love you."

"I love you too, Mom. Good night."

"Good night, Jamie."

Before she slipped into bed, Jamie picked up the book. She wanted to read again the account of the first Christmas in the New World. It was exciting to know that the night before Jesus was born in Bethlehem, he appeared to a person named Nephi in the New World and said: "*Lift up your head and be of good cheer; for behold, the time is at hand, and on this night shall the sign be given, and on the morrow come I into the world, to show unto the world that I will fulfil all that which I have caused to be spoken by the mouth of my holy prophets.*"

She lay in bed until midnight trying to figure out how to work that into her next conversation with her mom and dad.

There's so much to look forward to now, she thought, just before falling asleep.

PRELUDE TO A MISSION

After Kevin Overstreet's talk in sacrament meeting, after the open house for family and friends at his home after church, after the five-hour trip to Utah on Wednesday, after the tearful hugs and last good-byes at the MTC with his mom and dad and younger sister, Annie, and after being at the MTC for a week, Kevin woke up one morning feeling too guilty to go on—because he had not been honest in his interviews with his bishop and stake president.

It was not some slight oversight on his part, some small detail about his past he had neglected to bring up. He had purposely gone into his interviews planning to withhold information about his past. At the time it seemed like the best thing to do because if he told everything, they might not let him go on a mission. He didn't want to let everybody down; all his friends and family expected him to serve a mission.

On that night in August, when he'd shot out the tires on Brock Colby's pickup, he thought of it as settling an old score. But once he was at the MTC, where feelings about personal worthiness were heightened, he began to realize that what he had done was seriously wrong.

Brock Colby had been his enemy since the first time they'd met on a football field. They played opposite each other on the line. Even as a sophomore, Brock was

stronger, meaner, and more intimidating than anybody else
Kevin played against. On the first play of the first game of
their high school football careers, Brock hit Kevin so hard
his teeth rattled. "How'd you like that?" Brock had asked
as they lined up again.

"Like what?" Kevin said, trying his best to hide how
much he was hurting.

"Being hit by me."

"Oh, did you hit me? I didn't notice."

Brock, especially when he played football, had an evil
grin. "Well, I'll have to do better next time. By the time
this game is over you're going to be one big hurt."

"You ever notice some guys are all talk?" Kevin had
countered.

On the next play, Brock ran over Kevin, turned around,
and ran over him again.

The entire game was a nightmare for Kevin. It didn't
seem to matter what play was called. When the ball was
snapped, Brock took it as his job to inflict as much pain as
he could on Kevin.

Their teams played twice during the season. Nobody
on any other team manhandled Kevin as much or kept up
as steady a chatter of trash talk during a game as Brock
Colby.

After football season was over, both of them went out
for basketball. Kevin was much taller and more suited for
basketball. He enjoyed making Brock look bad.

The fierce rivalry continued the next year. In football
Kevin got smart enough and strong enough to give back as
much as he got. Brock countered by becoming the master
of the late hit or the elbow in the back when Kevin was
buried near the bottom of a pileup.

Kevin became curious about what his rival was like off
the field, and so he asked his cousin who went to the same

high school as Brock. He found out that Brock never went to church and that he drank on weekends and had such a bad reputation with girls at his school that most of them wouldn't go out with him. *It figures,* Kevin thought.

During their senior year, their rivalry got out of hand. The two teams played each other for the third time at the end of the season with the state title on the line. On one play, in the second quarter, Brock got past Kevin and did so much damage in sacking the quarterback that the dazed signal-caller had to be taken out of the game. After that, Kevin's team wasn't the same. They ended up losing the game 28 to 6. The only points they made the whole game came on two field goals.

Kevin felt bad for letting Brock get past him and so, in the first basketball game of the season, during one play where they both were fighting for the ball, Kevin saw his opportunity. He made it look as though he was going for the ball, then sent his elbow crashing into Brock's nose. Brock was bleeding so badly he had to sit out for several minutes, and while he was on the bench, Kevin scored twelve points. It was enough to win the game.

The second time they would have played against each other during the season, Brock wasn't on the team. Kevin found out he had been kicked out of school because of too many absences. Kevin was the high scorer for that game. He hoped Brock would find out about it.

Their animosity toward each other might not have gone any further and might only have been chalked up as a fierce sports rivalry. But it went beyond that the summer following Kevin's graduation. On the second Saturday in July he took Rachel Pearson to Rigby Lake. Kevin had talked his dad into buying a small sailboat from a neighbor. Rigby Lake was an ideal place to learn how to sail.

Kevin had been spending time with Rachel ever since

her family moved to town when she was a sophomore in high school. They got along well enough that they had begun to talk about getting married after Kevin returned from his mission.

He and Rachel had just launched the boat when Brock showed up with some of his friends. They acted as though they'd been drinking. "We need to get out of here as fast as we can," Kevin said privately to Rachel as they worked to get the sail up. It was the first time he'd ever tried to sail the boat, and he really didn't know what he was doing.

Five minutes later, they were still only twenty feet from shore when Brock sauntered onto the dock. "Well, look what we got here. You sail about as good as you play football, Overstreet. Maybe you should have set that thing up in your bathtub. Hey, come here, I want to talk to you."

"What for?"

"I haven't stomped on you lately."

"I don't think so, Brock. I could take you alone, but I'm not going to do it with all your friends around you."

"All right then, let's just talk about the good old days." He took a big gulp of beer, belched, and gave Kevin that ugly smile Kevin had grown to hate.

"There never were any good old days between us, Brock."

"They were good for me. I've missed pushing your face into the ground, so that's why I want you to come here."

Kevin was doing everything he could think of to make the boat move away from the dock, but there wasn't much of a breeze, so he wasn't having any luck. "Sorry, but you caught me at a bad time. I'm real busy now."

Rachel did not like violence or confrontation. "Don't even talk to him," she said softly.

The sound of her voice carried across the water. "Who's she?" Brock asked.

"Just a friend."

"How come she's spending time with a loser like you when she could be with a *real man,* like me?"

The wind picked up and because Kevin didn't know anything about sailing, they started moving toward the dock where Brock was standing. "You coming to see me, Overstreet? We'll have a good old time, just you and me and my tire iron. I think I'll rearrange your face. Couldn't turn out much worse than it is now, right?"

Kevin swung the sail over to the other side, and the boat slowly started to pull away from the dock.

"You're going the wrong way," Brock called out. "Hey, Sweetie, what's your name?"

No answer.

"No problem. I can look it up in the yearbook. I'll come visit you sometime when you're least expecting it. We'll have a good old time, just you and me."

Kevin stayed in the middle of the lake until he saw Brock's beat-up pickup leave. He thought the incident was over until a month later, when Rachel told him she had been having nightmares about Brock showing up at her house late at night. They were awful dreams, and it had gotten so bad she was afraid to even go to sleep.

That was when Kevin made up his mind that if he ever got a chance, he'd pay Brock back for scaring Rachel.

His chance came in August when he was working for his dad harvesting grain on a dryland farm they'd just bought. The farm was twenty miles from home, not far from where Brock lived. They'd had an equipment breakdown during the day, so Kevin had stayed later than usual helping to fix it. By the time he started for home, it was eleven-thirty at night. As he passed a scenic overlook, his headlights momentarily showed Brock's pickup parked there. It was easy enough to spot because it was the only one around with the hood painted with a bright yellow primer.

This is my chance, Kevin thought. He continued on until he rounded a bend and then pulled over and stopped. He grabbed his rifle from its mount behind his head and started walking back up the road. Whenever he heard a car coming, he jumped into the underbrush and hid until it passed.

Slowly he made his way to the pickup. He positioned himself to get a good shot at the two tires on the driver's side of the vehicle. He moved a little closer and waited. From the light of a passing car, he could see that Brock was in there with a girl.

Finally the road was clear. The truck's windows were open and he could hear Brock and his girlfriend arguing, but he couldn't make out what they were saying.

When Kevin shot the left rear tire, the girl inside the pickup screamed.

"Get down!" Brock yelled out to her.

"What happened?" the girl cried out.

"Somebody shot out one of my tires." He opened his door and swore into the night.

Then Kevin shot out the left front tire.

"Make them stop!" the girl cried out.

"What, and get myself killed?"

Kevin moved silently around the truck to where he could get a good view of Brock's other two tires.

"I have a gun too!" Brock shouted.

Kevin fired again trying to hit another tire but couldn't tell if he had or not. An instant later he heard a cow bellow.

Kevin stood up and ran quickly down the hill toward where he'd parked. Brock must have heard him because he shouted after him. "I'll get you for this! Nobody does that to me! Nobody!"

A light in a nearby farm house went on. Kevin ran faster. The cow was still bellowing. Kevin realized it was possible his bullet had accidentally struck the cow.

When Kevin made it to his pickup, he jumped in and started it and drove away without turning on his lights until he was out of sight.

Kevin halfway expected Brock might suspect it was him. All that night he waited nervously, thinking the police might come. He was prepared to lie, but nobody ever came to talk to him. Apparently Brock had many enemies.

The only thing Kevin ever saw about what had happened was in a newspaper article about a farmer who reported one of his prize bulls had been shot and killed in the field at night. A reward was offered for information leading to the arrest of the person who had done it.

Kevin was careful to cover up any possible evidence. He cleaned his rifle twice within the first two days after the shooting. And he never told anyone what he'd done.

Shortly after that Brock was picked up for DUI and lost his license. Kevin didn't see him around much after that.

When it came time to be interviewed for his mission, Kevin decided it wasn't necessary for him to admit what he'd done. He told himself it wasn't serious enough to waste the bishop's time.

The interview went well. The bishop was on Kevin's side. He was, in fact, Rachel's father. Kevin had spent many hours in their home. Kevin suspected the bishop would be happy if Rachel married him after his mission.

There were easy questions and there were hard questions, but at no time was Kevin asked if he'd ever shot out the tires of a pickup late at night when two people were in it, or if he'd ever shot and killed a man's bull . The only question that came even remotely close was, "Are you honest in your dealings with your fellowmen?"

Kevin focused his answer on school. He had never cheated on an exam. "Yes sir, I am."

The only other question that gave him any hesitation was, "Is there anything you've done in the past that you haven't discussed with a priesthood leader that you should talk about at this time?"

"Like what?" Kevin had asked.

"Something you feel guilty about."

I don't feel guilty about what I did to Brock, Kevin thought. *I was just paying him back for what he did to me.* "Not really."

The bishop must have sensed some hesitancy. "You're positive?"

"Yes, sir."

Kevin made it through the interviews with his bishop and stake president. He thought it was finished, but he had not known what it would be like in the MTC. There, even the best elders and sisters went through a period of intense self-evaluation. Their instructors emphasized over and over how important it is to be worthy to preach the gospel—that they could not serve effectively as a missionaries if anything had been left unresolved. For Kevin the guilt quickly became unbearable.

Finally, Kevin met with his branch president at the MTC and confessed everything. He expected to be told that what he had done was wrong. He would then say that he would never do it again. And then it would be taken care of. His branch president, however, said Kevin needed to meet with the mission president of the MTC.

"What for?"

"That's what needs to be done in cases like this. And then he'll need to talk to your stake president."

The next morning Kevin was called into the mission president's office.

"Elder Overstreet, I understand you have something we need to talk about. Why don't you start at the beginning, and we'll see if there is something we can do to help you."

Kevin rehearsed the whole story for the president, who listened attentively. As Kevin recounted the feelings he had toward Brock Colby and then described how he had shot out the tires on Brock's truck, it sounded like such a stupid thing to do that Kevin wondered what he could have been thinking. And when he admitted that one of his stray bullets had probably killed the bull, Kevin saw clearly how cowardly and destructive his actions had been. He was ashamed and felt unworthy to be a missionary. Tears streamed down his face.

President Adams didn't respond immediately. He sat quietly and waited for Kevin to regain his composure. Then he said, "Elder Overstreet, it takes a lot of courage to confess something like this, and I appreciate your candor. But it's clear to me that you can't go forward with your mission unless these matters have been fully resolved. I'm going to call your stake president and discuss it with him. You can wait in the office next door, and I'll invite you back in as soon as I have been able to contact him."

Wiping his eyes with a tissue from a box on the president's desk, Kevin went into an adjoining room. He sat down on a chair and wondered what was going to happen to him. He suspected there was a chance he might be sent home, but he didn't think that would happen.

After a time, the mission president opened the door to

the room where Kevin was waiting and invited him back into his office.

"I've spoken with your stake president, and we are in agreement," he said. "You need to go home and resolve the situation and further prepare yourself to serve. President Lawrence will call your parents and make arrangements to have them pick you up. Just as soon as they are able to come, you'll be excused to go home with them and begin working on the problem."

Kevin was stunned by what he was hearing. He thought about having to face his mom and dad. And he couldn't imagine what he'd say to Rachel or to his friends and ward members. He panicked. "Please don't send me home," Kevin pleaded.

"I'm sorry, but we have no choice."

"Why do you have no choice?"

"Because the police are looking for the person who shot that bull. How can you serve a mission when you're wanted by the police?"

"But it was an accident. I wasn't trying to kill the bull."

"That doesn't matter much, does it? The fact is, the bull is dead."

"No, this can't be. I want to serve a mission. That's all I've thought about since I was a little kid."

"We can't do anything further for you here. We'll hear from your parents soon."

As he walked to his room to pack his things, it was painful for Kevin to hear groups of missionaries practicing language skills and working on missionary discussions. They were a small army, and they were going out to change the world, but he was not going with them.

He knew what people at home said about missionaries who were sent home. There was no greater disgrace. And now people would talk about him like that. There would be speculation about why he'd been sent home. He knew that some of them would assume that he and Rachel had lost control. And so it wasn't just him. She would be talked about too. Morality was something he and Rachel had been careful about. But nobody would know that. They would all suspect the worst. And whenever he walked down the street, people would talk about him behind his back.

He wasn't the only one who would be affected by this. He knew how much his parents had wanted him to serve an honorable mission. And he had let them down. He wished he could run away and never see his parents again and never go home. But he had no money, and there was no place to go.

His parents showed up a little after six that evening. His father opened the trunk of the car and, like a movie running backward, Kevin returned his suitcases to the trunk.

They started for home. Nobody said much of anything until they approached Salt Lake City on I-15. And then his mother turned around and asked, "Kevin, do you want to talk about it?"

"Did they tell you why they're sending me home?"

"No, they didn't."

"It doesn't have anything to do with Rachel," he said quickly. "That's what you thought it would be, didn't you?"

"We didn't know *what* to think," his mother said.

"That's what everyone will think, though," Kevin said.

"We have no way of knowing what people will think," his father, always the realist, replied.

"Did it involve some other girl?" his mother asked. It was a painful question for her to even ask.

"No, it wasn't like that at all."

"Well, are you going to tell us or not?" his father asked abruptly. "Because I think we have a right to know."

"There's a guy I played against in football and basketball. We've never liked each other. He scared Rachel one time when we went sailing at Rigby Lake. I promised myself I'd pay him back for what he did to her. Last summer on my way home from the dry farm one night I saw his pickup parked on a hill. He was with a girl. I shot out two of his tires. My third shot must have hit somebody's bull and killed it. That's all there is to it."

His father's temper got the best of him. "How could you pull a stupid, idiotic stunt like that?"

"I couldn't let him get away with scaring Rachel."

"You know what?" his dad fumed. "They were right in sending you home. With an attitude like that, you have no business serving a mission."

"The mission president says if I can work it out with President Lawrence, then I can go back to the MTC."

"You'll work it out," his mother said. "I know you will."

"I can't believe you'd do something so stupid," his father raged. "What if you'd killed someone? Did you ever think about that?"

"I was real careful."

His dad was nearly out of control. "What's careful got to do with it? Once a bullet ricochets, you've lost control of where it's going. That does it. I'm selling your guns tomorrow."

"You have no right to do that. They're my guns."

"Not anymore, they're not. Do you realize you could end up going to jail for this? Some mission that'll be."

"Don't be so hard on him," his mother said softly.

"It looks to me like I haven't been half hard enough. You think you're making progress—you think you've got a

son with a little bit of common sense, and then he pulls
some harebrained stunt like this. I know what I'd do if I'd
lost a bull. I'd do everything I could to make sure you were
thrown in jail. That's what I'd do. I can't believe this."

Kevin spent the time staring out the window. When
his mother suggested they stop for something to eat, his
father grumbled, "We've got food at home." And then he
added bitterly, "No use wasting our money. We might
need all we've got for lawyers."

"Look, if it will make your life any easier, I'll plead
guilty," Kevin shot back. "That'll end up costing you less
money."

"You're not the only one in trouble here. They could
sue me, and then I'd end up losing everything."

Kevin did not say anything else for the rest of the trip.
They arrived back home around eleven that night.

"Could you please pull into the garage?" Kevin asked.

"What for?" his dad asked.

"I don't want any of the neighbors seeing me."

"What difference does it make?" his father said bitterly. "This is going to be all over town by tomorrow
anyway."

"David," his mother quietly chided his father.

"All right, all right. I'll pull inside."

They pulled into the garage. His mother reached over
to the sun visor and touched the control that closed the
garage door. His father, still so angry he did not trust himself to speak, went inside.

"Do you need any help?" his mother asked.

"No."

Kevin carried his things to his room. As he was hanging up his second suit, his younger sister, Annie, walked
into his room.

"Hello," she said tentatively. "Did you do something wrong?" she asked.

"Yes."

"It must have been really bad for them to send you home."

"It doesn't have anything to do with Rachel." He said it because Annie's best friend Ginger was Rachel's sister.

She paused. "Rachel knows about it already."

"How did she find out?"

"I had to call Ginger and tell her she couldn't have supper here after all, like we'd planned. She asked why, so I told her. She must have told Rachel because Rachel called me right back and asked if it was true. So she knows."

"Oh," Kevin said, shaking his head.

As Annie left, Kevin closed the door to his room and sat on the bed. He knew he should finish unpacking but knew that would be painful. He felt numb and weak.

When his mother came downstairs to his room and asked if he wanted something to eat, he told her he wasn't hungry.

A few minutes later he heard the phone ring. Then, after a few seconds, Annie came to his room. "President Lawrence is on the phone. He wants to talk to you."

"Can you bring the phone down here?" he asked.

"You can't stay down here forever," Annie said.

"Please."

"All right, I'll do it tonight, but don't expect it from now on."

She brought the portable phone to him. He thanked her and closed the door. "Hello," he said.

"Kevin, this is President Lawrence. I'd like to meet with you tomorrow morning at eight-thirty. How would that fit into your schedule?"

"Fine. Where at?"

"My office in the stake center."

Kevin got very little sleep that night. He dreaded leaving the house. He feared the knowing glances, the smirks, the questions he would be asked. There was nobody he could count on to be supportive. Most of his friends from high school were already on their missions; he didn't have anyone to talk to.

He wondered how Rachel would be treated. He knew she would be the subject of speculation about what they might have done that was serious enough for him to be sent home from his mission.

That morning he skipped breakfast and got dressed in his suit, one of his new white shirts, and a tie. He drove to the stake center. It was only two blocks; he could have walked, but he didn't want anyone to see him.

As he entered the stake center, he ran into a custodian. "I thought you just left on your mission," the man said.

Kevin didn't know how to respond. "Excuse me," he said.

If President Lawrence was disheartened about Kevin being sent home from the MTC, it was not apparent from his handshake or his smile. "Kevin, thank you for getting up so early to come and see me." He motioned for Kevin to sit down.

President Lawrence sat at his desk, glanced down at his notes, and then looked up. "Well, Kevin, apparently there's some unfinished business that needs to be taken care of. Is that right? Your mission president told me some things in general, but perhaps you can go through it for me in detail."

Kevin told him everything.

"It would have been best if you'd told your bishop

about this right after it happened," President Lawrence said.

"I know that, now."

"Or if you'd talked about it when you were inter-viewed for your mission, either to your bishop or to me."

"Yes, sir, I should have done that," Kevin said.

"I'm interested to know why you didn't."

"I don't know."

"Kevin, I don't mean to be unkind, but did you really think you could hide this from your Father in Heaven or from the Savior?"

Kevin turned away so President Lawrence wouldn't be able to see his eyes. The president placed a box of tissues within Kevin's reach. "If you're going to excommunicate me, then just do it, okay?" Kevin said.

"I'm sorry, Kevin. I know this is hard on you, but we have to get to the bottom before we can start back up again."

"Everyone is going to make fun of me," Kevin agonized.

"Is that what worries you the most?"

"I guess it is."

"What people might think is not the issue here. Worrying what people might think can be a bad thing sometimes, especially if it causes a person to try to cover up his mistakes."

"I just knew I wanted to go on a mission," Kevin said.

President Lawrence's eyebrows raised. "At any price?"

"I guess so."

"Do you know what the price is for covering something like this up?"

"No."

"It's the loss of the Spirit. You can't have the influence of the Holy Ghost if you're covering up your sins. And without the Holy Ghost, you can't be effective as a missionary. So, even if you'd gone ahead, your mission would have been a disaster, both for you and for the people you worked with. This is serious business, Kevin."

Kevin had no respect for men who showed emotion, and now he was doing it, and he hated himself even more for it.

"Kevin, let me ask you a question—do you believe in the atonement of Jesus Christ?"

"Yes, President, I do."

"Then why have you gone out of your way to avoid taking advantage of the Atonement?"

"What I did isn't so bad as some people I know who have already left on their missions."

"Are you saying they lied to their bishops and stake presidents?" President Lawrence asked.

"Yes."

"They'll be back, Kevin. Some of them will make it a year, some even longer, but their missions will be a heavy burden for them. And even for the ones who stay the full two years, unless they go through the repentance process, they will never catch fire. They will always be just going through the motions. There is no other way to find peace of mind except through the Savior. He is our only hope. He is our only salvation. So it does no good for you to lie to me in an interview. I'm not the one you need to concern yourself with. The one you need to please is the Savior. And the only way to please Him is for you to go through the repentance process. If you do that, you can be forgiven completely. That's what really counts."

"What's going to happen to me?" Kevin asked.

"That's up to you. I think we need to start from the beginning. I'd like to interview you again. This time I want you to be completely honest with me. Will you do that?"

"Yes, President, I'll be totally honest."

It was painful revealing things he had never confessed to anyone but should have in past interviews with his bishop. But he did it. He didn't hold back anything. And when it was finally all out, President Lawrence asked several questions about details and then asked, "Are you sure that's everything?"

Kevin went over in his mind the mistakes he'd made. *This must be what it will be like at the Judgment*, he thought. "Yes, that's everything."

"All right, good. Now, what you need to do is go through the process of repentance for those items that are still unresolved. And when that's done, we'll determine if it is possible to send you back out on your mission."

Kevin experienced a glimmer of hope.

President Lawrence explained what needed to be done. "First, you must visit with the farmer whose bull you killed and this other boy, Brock, and the girl he was with. You must satisfy them first before anything else can happen."

Kevin's hope again plunged downward. "Why do I have to do that?"

President Lawrence turned to the scriptures. "This is from Matthew, chapter five. Please read verses 23 and 24."

"Out loud?"

"Yes, please."

Kevin began reading. "Therefore if thou bring thy gift to the altar, and there rememberest that thy brother hath ought against thee; Leave there thy gift before the altar, and go thy way; first be reconciled to thy brother, and then come and offer thy gift."

"Your gift is your mission," President Lawrence

explained. "You need to be reconciled with those you have injured before you can serve a mission. Will you do that?"

"If you want me to, I will."

President Lawrence cleared his throat. Kevin, these are not my rules. It is the Savior you need to satisfy."

"There's something else we have to do. Tomorrow morning you and I will go to sacrament meeting in your ward. After the sacrament I will talk for a few minutes. I will tell the members of the ward that there are a few things you need to work out before you are able to continue with your mission. I will tell them I support you in what you are trying to do, and then, I will turn some time to you for you to bear your testimony."

Kevin winced. He closed his eyes and shook his head. "Why do we have to do that?"

"Because your ward has a right to know why you're home. If we let them know, right from the first, then there will be no room for rumors."

Kevin shook his head again. "That will be hard."

"I know, Kevin, but it needs to be done. Look, you're on the road to repentance. You're better off right now than you've been for a long time."

"I'm worried there will be gossip about me and Rachel."

"I'll put that to rest when I talk to your ward."

After the interview was over, Kevin drove around on some back roads for a couple of hours. He thought about what he needed to do and how he was going to face everyone at church on Sunday.

When he finally returned home, he drove into the garage, shut the door, and then got out of the car. As he walked into the house through the garage entrance, Annie called out, "Rachel called. She wants you to call her back."

She tried to hand him the phone. He shook his head.

"Aren't you going to call her?" Annie asked.

"No."

"Why not?"

"I can't talk to her yet."

He went to his room, closed the door, and sat on his bed and looked at himself in the mirror. He was still wearing one of the suits his parents had bought for him to wear on his mission. But it didn't matter now. He could wear anything because he wasn't a missionary anymore.

He dreaded seeing Rachel. She had always told him what a good missionary he was going to be.

His mother came down to see him. "How did it go this morning?"

"Okay, I guess. There's still a chance I can go on my mission."

"That's wonderful. You'll work it out. I know you will. Come on up for lunch now."

"I'm not hungry."

"You need to eat. I've fixed some sandwiches."

"Not now."

His mother left.

Kevin went into the bathroom and splashed water on his face and brushed his teeth. He felt tired and overwhelmed, but he needed to go talk to Brock and the girl who'd been with him in the pickup that night and to the farmer. That was the most important thing now.

His father thundered down the stairs carrying a tuna sandwich and a glass of milk. "Eat this now and quit all this foolishness. You've got your mother worried sick."

At times Kevin's father got a certain look that said don't mess with me. He had that look now. Kevin took the plate and the milk and set them down on the counter in the bathroom. His father was still glaring at him; Kevin took a bite of the sandwich. "I have to go talk to the farmer who owned the bull and to the guy whose tires I shot out and the girl who was with him that night. President Lawrence told me I need to square things with them first."

"You planning on going alone?"

"Yeah."

"I think I'd better go with you."

"Why?"

"I might be able to talk to the farmer. And I don't want you talking to that hotheaded kid alone. You might end up killing each other."

"You don't have to come with me."

His dad wasn't in the mood to bargain. "There are a lot of things I don't have to do, but this isn't one of them. You'd better change first."

Kevin changed into working jeans and a button shirt, like his dad was wearing. His father drove. They didn't either one of them say much.

It took three tries before they found the right farm. They walked, father and son, up the path to the front door of the farmhouse. Kevin knocked on the door.

Kevin had hoped the man was an active member of the Church and more likely to forgive someone who wanted to serve a mission, but the man came to the door with a cigarette in his mouth. "Yeah, whataya want?" he growled.

Kevin wondered if his dad would make it easy for him and explain everything, but after an uncomfortable silence he realized that wasn't going to happen.

"Well?" the man said impatiently.

"I'm the one who shot your bull," Kevin blurted out.

The man unleashed a string of swearwords at Kevin then turned to Kevin's father. "And who are you?"

"I'm his father. We're here to do what we can to make it up to you."

"It's chumps like us who always end up cleaning up the messes our kids make. Ain't that right?"

"A lot of times, that's what happens," Kevin's dad said.

"Well, this time it ain't going to come cheap."

His father nodded slowly. "We'll do whatever it takes."

The man pointed a stubby finger at Kevin's dad. "I don't want you bailing him out. No sir, that'd be too easy."

"I'll make sure he works for whatever it takes to make it right with you."

"You know—the best thing might be for him to spend some time in jail. I can press charges, you know."

"I guess that's up to you."

The man glared at Kevin. "I could do it too. Don't think I couldn't."

"If he's in jail, he won't be able to earn the money to pay you back."

The man nodded. "Well, that's a point. You know, if you ask me, kids these days have it too easy. That's the trouble with 'em."

"I've tried to teach my son right, but you never know what they're going to do."

"That's for sure. Say, what do you do for a living?"

"I farm," Kevin's father said.

"Is that a fact? Where at?"

"On the Rexburg bench. Also, I've got a dryland farm not too far from here."

"Where?"

"You know Hansen's old place? I'm taking part of that over."

"Hansen never could make a go of it. You'll be lucky to break even."

"We're hoping to do a little better than that."

The man, staring at Kevin's father, nodded slowly, as if he could relate with him now. "Come on in, and I'll try to figure out how much I'll need to get me another bull as good as the one your boy shot."

By the time they left the man's house, Kevin's father had written a check for the amount agreed upon and given it to the man, promising that Kevin would work until he paid it all back. For that the man agreed not to press charges.

Half an hour later they found the place where Brock lived. Brock's mother said he was sleeping, even though it was by then two in the afternoon. Kevin asked if she could get her son up.

They waited outside. Kevin's dad went and sat in the pickup with the door open. Kevin leaned against a tree and waited.

Ten minutes later Brock came out wearing jeans and a T-shirt, barefoot but carrying his shoes and socks.

"What's on *your* mind?" he asked, sitting on the porch steps to put on his shoes and socks.

"I was the one who shot out your tires," Kevin said.

That ugly grin came across Brock's face. "No kidding," he said, thoughtfully. "I didn't even suspect you. Guess I should've known."

"I came to apologize," Kevin said. "I'd like to make it up to you."

Brock pulled a knife from his pocket, opened it up, and ran his thumb across its edge. He flashed Kevin that impudent smile again. "What did you have in mind to do?"

"I'm willing to pay for the tires I shot out."

Brock ran the back of his hand across his mouth. "Really? Well, they were pretty good tires. About two hundred dollars a tire as I remember it."

"Show me the sales slip for the tires, and I'll pay it," Kevin said.

"You know, I think I threw the sales slip away. I guess you'll just have to take my word."

Kevin's dad stepped out of the pickup. "We'll pay whatever is fair. You say."

"Is this your dad?" Brock asked.

"Yeah."

"Why'd you bring him? Afraid to come here alone?"

Kevin's father took a step in Brock's direction. "I came to make sure you get whatever you need to square things up with my son."

Brock turned to Kevin. "How come you're just now coming to tell me about this?"

"I want to go on a mission."

Brock saw a weakness he needed to probe. "Are you saying I can stop you from going on a mission?"

"Yeah, you can."

"Well, that's easy then. We can't have you leaving here. You and me got some scores to settle."

Kevin's father took another step toward Brock. "We came here to make the situation right. Kevin needs to do this so he can get on with his mission."

"Well, that just about brings tears to my eyes," Brock said, then started laughing.

"What's so funny?" Kevin asked.

"I just remembered that those tires actually cost me four hundred apiece."

"We'll pay that now, but only if that's the end of it," Kevin's father said.

Brock came up to Kevin and smiled. "Looks like I'm going to come out okay on this deal, don't it? But then I always did better than you, didn't I?"

Kevin looked at his dad and shrugged, as if to say he was willing to pay Brock's price.

Kevin's father wrote out a check for eight hundred dollars and handed it to Brock.

"There was a girl in the truck with you that night. I need to talk to her too."

"She's inside. We're married now. I'll go get her."

A minute later a young woman came out with Brock. She had long dark hair and a pretty face.

"I was the one who shot out Brock's tires that night. You were in the pickup with him, weren't you?"

"I sure was. Man, you nearly scared me to death."

"I came to apologize. I'm sorry I scared you."

"That's not all he came for," Brock said. "Tell her," he said to Kevin.

"I'd like to try to make restitution for what I did."

"What he's trying to say," Brock interrupted, "is how much money do you want him to give you?"

"He said he was sorry," the girl said. "That ought to be enough."

"No, that's not enough. Don't you see? We have him over a barrel. He wants to go on a mission, but he can't go until he gets us satisfied. That means he and his dad are our own private money machine."

"But if he's going on a mission, I don't want anything from him."

"Look, maybe you don't understand what's going on here," Brock said. "You just name your price and Kevin's nice daddy will write out a check for that amount. You can get a washer or a dryer or whatever you want with the money."

"He just wants to go on a mission, Brock, that's all. I say we should let him go."

"She'd like two hundred dollars," Brock said. "Isn't that right, Babe?"

"I said I didn't want anything, and I meant it."

Brock looked angry. "Sometimes she's got a mind of her own. I guess that's it then, huh? So why don't you two get off our land before I change my mind and call the sheriff."

On the way home his dad didn't say anything for ten miles and then he glanced over at Kevin. "I hope you're not thinking I'm going to let you waltz out of here without working off what you owe me for all this."

"Is that what you think I'd do?" Kevin asked.

"I just want to make sure we understand each other. I figure you owe me about three months' work."

"Fine. I'll work for you as long as you want me to."

"Three months is about right. I know you want to get on your mission as soon as you can."

They rode in silence for a few more minutes. Then Kevin asked, "Do you think I should still plan on going on a mission?"

"I've always thought you'd be a good missionary. I still think that." He paused. "Maybe you can even learn a few things from this that'll help you be a better missionary."

Ever since Kevin was twelve years old and had started working with his dad, whenever he messed up, he'd heard the same thing over and over again from his father—"I just hope this will teach you a lesson." Kevin had come to dread those words. But this time, the way his father said it made it different. "What do you think I should learn from this?" Kevin asked.

"Well, for one thing, when you make a mess, you can't just walk away from it. You have to take care of it right away."

"I've learned that. What else?"

"I hope you can see now that you wouldn't have been much of a missionary if you'd left with this unresolved. And that none of us is ever going to amount to a hill of beans by ourselves. For my money, that's the most important thing for a missionary to know. By the time this is over, you'll probably know that better than most."

Kevin nodded. "You're right about that."

There was a long pause and then his dad asked, "Am I too hard on you?"

Kevin just shrugged his shoulders. "I guess I had it coming."

"Your mother thinks I am. She might be right. I don't mean to be, though. It's just the way I was brought up."

"It's okay, Dad. Really. Don't worry about it."

They entered the outskirts of town.

"Anyone else you need to see?" his dad asked. "Because I think we should get this over with so there's nothing else hanging over our heads. And then we can get on with life."

Kevin found it comforting that his father was sharing his burden. "I wasn't completely truthful in my interview with the bishop."

"All right, let's go see him. Who else?"

"Rachel. I never lied to her, but I have let her down."

"Let's take care of all that now."

A short time later his father pulled into the bishop's driveway. Kevin opened the door, stepped out, and started up the driveway.

His dad opened the driver-side door and leaned out. "Son?"

Kevin stopped in his tracks. His father had never before called him *son*. And the way he said it was different too; there was a gentleness in his voice Kevin had seldom heard before. Tears welled up in Kevin's eyes. He turned around to face his dad.

"Do you want me to come in with you?"

"No," Kevin said. "I can do it myself. Thanks anyway,

though. You don't have to wait for me if you don't want to. I'll walk home when I'm done."

"I don't mind waiting. I've got nothing else to do that's as important as this."

For just an instant they made eye contact, and Kevin sensed the depth of his father's love. "Dad?"

"What?"

"I'm glad I came back to straighten everything out. Thanks for your help today. I couldn't have done it without you."

His father nodded and turned away, hiding his eyes from his son.

Kevin continued up the driveway. In a few minutes it would all be done.

And then he could start over again.

ALL WE NEED
IS A SMALL ROOM

"I still don't see why I had to come," Brittany Spaulding complained as they waited in the Idaho Falls airport for her cousin Ryan's flight to arrive. Because of the late-November snowstorm, it had taken the Spauldings longer than usual to drive from their home in Driggs. "I mean, I hardly even know him."

"I'm sure he'll have questions about school," her mother said.

Brittany was in a bad mood. "There are a few things I'd like to know about him too—like how many people he's killed."

"He hasn't killed anyone and you know it," her mother said.

"Oh, really? I thought that's why you invited him to come stay with us."

Her mother went through it again. "Ryan started help-ing a girl with her homework in the library during lunch hour. She was going with a member of a gang. Someone saw them together, and, well, the gang member found out and got jealous and decided to teach Ryan a lesson. Last night three of them caught Ryan on the street."

"And that's when he killed somebody, right?" Brittany said.

"Stop it," her mother warned.

"We don't know all the details," her father continued, "but there was a fight, and when it was over, one of the boys was lying on the street with a stab wound. Before the police arrived and everyone scattered, one of the gang members threatened to kill Ryan the next time he saw him."

"So Ryan killed him," Brittany said.

"Just ignore her," her mother said.

Her father had more patience with Brittany than her mother. "No. Ryan ran home and told his parents what had happened. They didn't see how he could stay there anymore, so they called your mother and asked if he could stay with us the rest of his senior year."

"And of course Mom said yes without getting anyone else's opinion," Brittany said.

"I would have talked to you, but you weren't home, and they needed an answer right away. They were afraid to have him stay there even one more day."

"So you said, 'Sure, no problem. In fact, Ryan can take Brittany's room. She won't mind.'"

"He can't room with either you or Sarah, so what do you suggest?" her mother asked.

"Why can't he sleep on the couch?" Brittany asked.

"He needs his privacy."

"Oh sure, and I don't, right?"

"It won't kill you to be in with Sarah."

Brittany rolled her eyes. "My senior year?"

"I don't mind having Brittany stay in my room," Sarah said. She was only ten years old and still wanted to please everybody.

"Thank you, Sarah, I appreciate your cooperation," their mother said.

Brittany was not intimidated by being unfavorably

compared to Sarah. "So what else of mine did you give away?" she asked.

"Nothing else. Look, I'm sorry we don't have a bigger house."

"Not as sorry as I am right now."

"What did you want me to tell your aunt, that we wouldn't help?" her mother asked.

That would have been Brittany's first choice, but she didn't dare say it because, even to her, it sounded too heartless. She had nothing against Ryan personally. They had met for the first time at a family reunion three years before. His family lived in Chicago, and they didn't get out west much.

A short time later Ryan's flight was announced. In a few minutes, passengers began coming into the terminal. It was easy to spot Ryan because he was six foot four and had to duck coming through the door. Brittany's impression of him was that, with a little effort, he could look better than he did. His hair was cut brutally short. His cheekbones stood out, partly because of genetics and partly because he had long ago run off any extra weight that would add fullness to his features. The area around his right eye was black-and-blue and puffy, either from his fight in the street the night before or else from somebody's elbow in a basketball game.

Brittany remembered her mother saying what a good basketball player Ryan was. He'd had an outstanding sophomore and junior year at his high school in Chicago and was expected to have a great senior season. Several colleges had begun recruiting him to play. But now he had been forced to leave school.

As they walked out to the parking lot, Brittany critically picked up on what she interpreted as an overly confident swagger.

Then, while stowing his luggage in the trunk, Brittany's mother asked, "Ryan, why don't you sit in front?"

"No, that's okay, I can sit in back," he said.

"I know, but you're pretty tall. I think you'll be much more comfortable in front."

"Well, all right, thanks a lot."

Brittany ended up crammed in the back with her mother and Sarah while Ryan stretched out in the front seat.

On the long ride home, made worse by blowing snow on the highway, everything focused on Ryan. Brittany sat in the backseat and made a mental list of the things she didn't like about him. The first was that he spoke like a Mid-Westerner. The second was that he didn't seem scared or even uncomfortable.

When they arrived home, Brittany's mother showed Ryan around the house. "This will be your room. I hope it will be all right."

"It'll be just great. Thanks a lot."

Brittany pushed her way through the doorway, past her mother and Ryan. "Excuse me, I have a few more things I need to get," she said.

"Is this your room?" Ryan asked.

"Not anymore," Brittany said, trying not to sound so bitter that her mother would get after her.

"Hey, I don't want to take your room," Ryan said.

"Brittany will be fine," her mother said. "She'll be in with Sarah. They've roomed together before."

"Yeah, right, up until the seventh grade," Brittany muttered. She went to the closet, grabbed her shoes from the floor, dumped them into a wastebasket, and made a big show of it as she hauled them out.

"Thanks for giving up your room," Ryan said as she breezed past him.

"Don't thank me, thank my mother," Brittany said. It was her parting shot.

The next morning Brittany drove Ryan to school and showed him to the principal's office. Then, because she had classes of her own, she abandoned him.

She didn't see him again until lunchtime. She was standing in the food line when he came over to her. "Is it okay if I eat with you?" he asked.

"I usually eat with my friends," she said coolly.

"Well, could you make an exception just for today?"

She sighed. He was, after all, her cousin. "Yeah, sure."

"Thanks."

Brittany always had lunch with Julia, Diane, and Amanda. She couldn't believe how much they fussed over Ryan—especially Diane. She sat next to him, gave him her dessert, and, once, she leaned against him after he kidded her about something.

When Ryan finished eating, he looked at the clock and said, "I need to talk to the basketball coach about playing for him this year."

"I don't think they need anybody. They already have a good team," Brittany said.

"With me, they'll be even better," he said, grinning.

She hated his smile. It was like he always expected good things to happen to him.

Brittany and Ryan had arranged to meet at her locker after school, so she could give him a ride home. When he showed up, he said, "I've got basketball practice now, so I won't be going home with you."

"So how are you getting home?"

He hesitated. "Could you come and get me at five-thirty?"

"I'm not running a free taxi service here, you know. You got any money for gas?"

"Look, if it's a problem, I'll walk home," he said.

They lived two miles away. She gave a pained sigh. "I suppose I could pick you up—but just this once."

Brittany called her mother and told her about Ryan wanting a ride home after basketball practice. "I guess I'll go to the library and work on a report that's due next week."

She worked on the report until five-fifteen and then decided to drop by and watch the practice. She was good friends with three of the seniors on the team. They had sat on the bench through much of their junior year, all the while hoping that their senior year would be their time to shine.

By the time Brittany showed up, the coach had realized how good Ryan was. He had Ryan on the floor along with two of the seniors while Austin Aldredge, the third senior, sat on the bench and watched his high school career going down the drain. With Ryan on the team, he wasn't going to get much playing time.

"Great move, Ryan, way to play heads-up ball," the coach called out.

He's ruining everything, Brittany thought. *He's taken over my room. He's taking over my friends. By the end of the month he'll take over the school, and people like Austin and me will end up on the sidelines totally ignored.*

She spotted Diane sitting in the bleachers on the other side. *We used to be such good friends,* she thought, *but Ryan's coming between us. Pretty soon I won't have any friends.*

After the coach called an end to practice and sent everybody to the showers, Ryan stayed and shot a few baskets. Several guys on the team, including the coach, lingered behind and watched as Ryan swished eight out of

ten three-point shots from all over the court. When he finished, Ryan retrieved the ball, looked around, and realized
people were watching. "Just lucky, I guess," he said.
Nobody believed him.

Brittany and Diane waited in the hall for Ryan to come
out of the locker room. Diane couldn't stop talking about
him.

"I hope you know you're making a complete fool of
yourself," Brittany said.

"That's my business, isn't it?"

"You think he likes you? Well, you can forget that. The
only person he really cares about is himself."

"You and he must have a lot in common then, right?"
Diane said.

"What's that supposed to mean?"

"You're not making it very easy for him."

"I gave up my room for him. What more do you want?"

"You're so mean to him."

"What are you talking about?"

"The way you look at him, the way you talk to him."

"Can't you see what he's doing?" Brittany asked. "He's
one of those pushy eastern types. You just wait. Before you
know it, he'll take over the whole school."

"Good, I hope he does," Diane said.

"Look, when he comes out of the locker room, then he
and I are leaving. So whatever you have to say to him,
you'd better say it fast, because I'm not waiting around."

At first Diane hesitated to say anything because she
knew what Brittany was like when she got mad. "Look, if
you're in so much of a hurry, I might be able to help out.
I've got my mom's car today . . . so I could take him
home."

"Well, this is a great time to tell me that. I've only
been sitting around here for three hours. Give it up,

Diane; he's not interested in you, so you might as well forget it."

"Well, maybe so, but I'm sure I'd be better company for him on the way home than you will. Are you planning on biting his head off, too, like you're doing with me?"

She threw up her hands. "I give up! You want to take him home? Fine, be my guest. But let me warn you—we eat at six. You make sure he's home on time." She stormed out of the building and drove too fast on her way home.

Much to Brittany's disappointment, Ryan did arrive home on time.

As they ate supper, Ryan told them it looked like he had made the team. Her parents and Sarah ate it up. Brittany wondered if anyone would ask her how *her* day had been—but they didn't. They were too wrapped up in Wonder Boy.

"Oh, there is one other thing," Ryan said. "Is it okay if I call home?"

"Of course, anytime," her mother said. "Is it anything we can help you with?"

"Well, not really. I just need to ask my parents to send me some money. The coach told me to get some new shoes for basketball. Mine are pretty beat up."

"Are you in a hurry for the shoes?" Brittany's father asked.

"Well, kind of, but I can get by with my old ones until then."

Brittany's father had played basketball in high school and, even now, went to most of the home games. "Let us take care of it. Your parents have enough to worry about with your younger brothers. Let this be an early Christmas present from us."

A week earlier Brittany had asked for a snowboard for Christmas and had been told they were too expensive.

I should've been a boy, she thought bitterly—*a tall, pushy boy with big feet and a banged-up face. If I'd been a boy like Ryan, I could have anything I want.*

"So why don't we go right after we finish eating?" her father suggested.

"That'd be really great. Thanks a lot."

Her mother and Sarah also needed to do some shopping. "Brittany, could you do the dishes while we're gone?" her mother asked just before she joined the others in the car.

"Is Ryan ever going to help out around here, or are you planning on making me the permanent family slave?"

"He'll do his part too."

"I don't believe that," Brittany said.

"We can talk about this later, but for now will you please do the dishes? It is your turn, you know."

"Sure, whatever you say," she grumbled. *Maybe you'd like me to wash Ryan's grungy gym clothes too,* she thought bitterly. *I mean, after all, we have to keep our boy happy now, don't we?*

After she finished the dishes, she went into what used to be her room, but it wasn't hers anymore. Ryan had taken over. He was here to stay. He was taking over her place in the family, and there wasn't a thing she could do about it.

She needed to talk to someone who would understand how she felt, so she called Austin Aldredge. "So Austin, how was basketball practice tonight?" she asked.

"You were there; you know how it was. Ryan is your cousin, isn't he? Why's he here, anyway?"

"Promise not to tell anyone, okay?" she asked, knowing full well Austin couldn't keep a secret.

"Yeah, sure."

This was her chance to get back at Ryan. "He's from

Chicago. He was in a gang, and I guess he got in a fight and killed a guy with a knife."

"If he killed somebody, how come he's not in jail?"

"No proof."

"Why'd he come here?" Austin asked.

"Some friends of the guy he killed were after him, so he had to get out of town. Oh, but look, you have to promise not to say anything, because he wants to start a whole new life out here."

"Yeah, sure, no problem."

When she hung up, she was surprised that she didn't feel any better. She thought she would.

A few minutes later the phone rang. It was the ward activity committee chairman. "Brittany, is that you? I'm glad I caught you. We need your help." Sister Harris was a friendly, bubbly kind of person. "The ward is doing a nativity scene for the ward Christmas party, and I'd like your family to help us with it," she gushed. "I especially want you to play the part of Mary."

"I'm really busy."

"We'll practice just once the night before, and you won't have any lines to memorize."

"Why me?"

"Because it's easy for me to imagine you as Mary."

"Why?"

"Well, because you have long brown hair, and that's the way I picture Mary. But more than that even, I just think you fit the part."

She didn't feel like it at that moment. "I don't think I'm the right person."

"Please, I really need you and your family."

Brittany sighed. It didn't sound like it would take too much time. "All right, I'll do it. But you'd better talk to my mom about the rest of the family."

"I'll do that. Thanks a lot, Brittany. The ward party is in a couple of weeks. I think it'll be all right if we just practice once that week."

Within the next few days rumors about Ryan raced through school and became more distorted with each telling. Now some people were saying that Ryan had killed three guys in a fight.

The coach heard the rumors and called Ryan's former basketball coach, only to find out that Ryan was innocent of any wrongdoing.

He tried his best to stop the gossip, but it didn't seem to do any good.

Ryan earned the right to play first-string on the team. At the first game he played, he was booed by students from both schools. But nobody could accuse Ryan of not being able to play basketball. He scored 33 points, had seven rebounds, and blocked five shots.

Sunday afternoon after church, Ryan came in the kitchen and sat down with Brittany. Everyone else was taking a nap. "Somebody's spreading lies about me."

"Like what?" she asked.

"They're saying I killed some people before I came here. Somebody even told me they'd heard I'd cut up a girl pretty bad. Have you heard anything like that at school?"

"Not really."

His shoulders were slumped and his gaze fixed on the floor. "I try to act like it doesn't matter," he said softly, "but it does. I don't know if I can stay here much longer. I'm thinking about going home."

"But wouldn't you be in danger if you went home?"

"Probably. But at least back home I know who my enemies are."

"Excuse me, I'll be right back." Brittany left the room

and went into the bathroom and ran some cold water over her face and then dried it. And then she brushed her teeth. Her heart was pounding and her face was still red and the T-shirt she was wearing was damp with perspiration. She went into the room she shared with Sarah and changed shirts and then she returned to the kitchen where Ryan was reading the paper, waiting for her.

"I think you should stay here," she said. "I'm pretty sure things will get better."

Brittany considered telling Ryan that she was the one who had started the rumors, but she decided not to because she thought she could take care of it quietly without Ryan even knowing.

Later that day, while Ryan was over at Diane's house, Brittany phoned Austin and told him that what she'd said about Ryan was a lie. "You've got to help me stop all the bad things people are saying about Ryan. None of it is true, and it's really starting to get to him. He's thinking about leaving."

"Gosh, that'd be too bad if he left, wouldn't it?" Austin said sarcastically.

She knew she wasn't going to get any help from Austin.

On Monday at school, Brittany did everything she could to stop the rumors by talking to people and telling them the truth. But nothing she said seemed to make any difference. The stories had a life of their own.

On Wednesday, Diane's parents learned what people were saying about Ryan. They refused to let Diane spend any more time with him, even warning her that if she tried to see him behind their backs they'd send her to live with her aunt in Denver. Diane had no choice. She quit seeing him, although, when her parents left the house, she still talked to him on the phone.

Ryan denied everything people said about him, but nobody believed him. Around school he became quieter and less sure of himself, and he was not so quick with a smile anymore.

On Thursday night, Brittany passed his room. Ryan had closed the door, but the latch didn't catch unless you practically slammed it. The door was partly open. She looked in and saw him wearing the sweats he used as pajamas, kneeling by his bed. He was praying.

I'm responsible for him feeling miserable, she thought. She felt bad about it but didn't know what she could do to make it better. She hoped the rumors would eventually die down.

The next week was the last week before Christmas break. It was a busy time for Brittany. She was senior class vice-president and in the school choir. She also played cello in the orchestra. She performed in three concerts that week and had two tests to study for. She stayed up past midnight Tuesday and Wednesday nights studying for tests. She didn't have much time to worry about Ryan. It was better that way.

The ward Christmas party was scheduled for Friday at six. The only time they could find to practice for the nativity scene was Thursday night. The family talked about their participation while they ate supper that evening. Brittany's dad was going to be the innkeeper and her mom would be his wife. Ryan had been asked to play the part of Joseph, and Brittany was to be Mary. Sarah would be a lamb in the stable. And the boys from the deacons quorum were to be the shepherds.

Because when she was with him it made her feel guilty, Brittany had spent the week avoiding Ryan. And now to be with him in a play was bad enough, but to be playing the part of the mother of Jesus made it even worse. "I really don't want to do this," she said to her mom.

"It's too late now to get anyone else," her mother said. "But look, it won't be that bad. You don't have to say anything. All you have to do is walk across the stage with Ryan, stand while the innkeeper tells you there's no room for you in the inn, then go to the stable. They'll turn the lights down. And when they come back on, you'll be looking down at a doll lying in a manger. You can do that, can't you?"

"I guess so," she said quietly.

An hour later, while they were on stage at the church practicing the manger scene, there was a power outage. "How long is this going to take?" Brittany impatiently asked Sister Harris.

"I hope not very long. Why do things like this happen at the worst times?"

There was nothing to do but wait. The only light in the cultural hall came from the battery-operated exit signs.

The family sat on bales of hay at the manger scene and waited. "Brittany," her mother asked, "what's it like to play the part of Mary?"

"I don't know. I haven't thought about it much. I'll just be glad when it's over."

"I've been thinking about Mary," her mother said. "Of course, we don't know all the details, so anything we say is speculation, but still I can't help wondering how it was for her. We know that when Joseph and Mary went to Bethlehem, it was close to the time for her to have her baby. How did she ever make that trip? Each jar and jolt in the road must have been painful for her. While they were looking for a place to stay, she must have worried if there'd be any privacy at all for her when she had her baby, and wondered who would help her."

"To tell you the truth, I haven't really felt much like Christmas this year," Brittany said.

"Why's that?" her mother asked.

"I don't know. Too busy, I guess."

"We've all been busy," her father said. "It's easy to get so busy you miss things that are the most important. I'm afraid I'm guilty of that too sometimes."

Through years of family home evenings Brittany had grown used to listening to her father talk about religion. Sometimes she tuned him out when he started in like this, or else she asked how long he was going to take because she had a lot of homework. But here in the darkness there was no place to go, and no excuses to make, so she listened to her father's calm, even voice.

"I wonder if the innkeeper had any idea what was happening that night. He may have missed the whole thing. He probably had a lot on his mind. There were so many travelers in town, and they all needed food and drink and provisions for their animals. We don't know exactly what happened, but in my mind I picture his wife or some other woman taking pity on Mary and making sure she at least had a roof over her head."

Brittany's dad went on. "I wonder if the innkeeper felt he was too busy to get involved in Joseph and Mary's problems. Wouldn't that have been a tragedy? The most important event in the history of the world, and he's counting change. If he missed it, then, when the crowds left, all he had to show for it was a little money. But he could have had so much more.

"I think that can happen to us now. If we're not careful, we can get so busy we lose track of what's most important. Sometimes we can get so busy we don't stop to help the people around us who need our help."

"One thing for sure, you've helped me when I needed it," Ryan said in the darkness. "I'll never be able to thank you enough for letting me come here. Especially Brittany, for giving up her room for me and helping me get started in school."

Tormented by her conscience, Brittany stood up. "I can't do this."

"What's wrong?" her mother asked.

"I can't talk about it now," Brittany said. "I'm going home."

"Who will play Mary?" her father asked.

"I don't know, but it won't be me. Get someone else."

"How will you get home?" her father asked.

"I'll walk."

"It's too cold out," her mother said.

"I don't care. I'm going anyway."

"I don't understand what's gotten into you," her mother said, "but if you're so bent on going home, I'll drive you."

In the car, on their way home, her mother asked, "Brittany, what on earth is going on?"

"Nothing."

"Do you expect me to believe that?" her mother asked.

"I don't want to talk about it."

"Whatever it is, we can work it out. But you've got to tell me what's bothering you."

Just before they pulled into the driveway, Brittany said, "I've done something really awful."

"Tell me what it was."

"It's really bad."

"I can't help you unless I know what it is."

She talked fast to get it over with. "I made up lies

about why Ryan came here and now nobody wants to have anything to do with him. And it's all because of me."

Her mother couldn't believe it. "You deliberately told lies about Ryan?"

Brittany slumped over and started to cry. "Yes," she moaned.

"How could you do such a cruel thing to your own cousin?"

"When he first came, I was so mad at you for telling him he could come without talking to me and for giving him my room. I guess I wanted to get back at him. I told one person, and now it's gone all over school. You should see how they treat him. He's totally alone, and it's all my fault."

"If you were mad at me, why didn't you come to me about it instead of taking it out on him?"

"I don't know."

"I can't believe you'd do something like that. What are you going to do about it?"

"It's too late to do anything."

"You have to do something." There was a long silence. "Don't you?"

She turned to look at her mother. "I've tried to stop the rumors, but nothing I say seems to make any difference."

There was a pause and then her mother spoke slowly. "I think you need to admit to everyone that you were the one who started the rumors."

"I can't do that. It's asking too much. This is my senior year. If I say anything, I'll end up without any friends."

"If you don't say anything, it will be worse in the long run."

"I can't do it, so don't even ask me."

"I think you can. But you think about it and tell me what you've decided in the morning."

Brittany got out of the car and trudged into the house. Her mother returned to the practice.

When the family came home, Brittany waited in her room a few minutes and then knocked on Ryan's door. He opened it.

"Can I talk to you?" she asked.

They went into the kitchen, and she told him everything. He didn't react much to what she had to say. She couldn't read how he might be feeling.

When she finished, he asked quietly, "Was it because I took your room?"

"No."

"Not at all?"

"No, of course not. This wasn't about some dumb room. This was about me. It's time I faced the truth about myself. Sometimes I'm not a very good person. I try to be but then something happens, and I mess up, and I know I'm in the wrong, but it's like I can't do anything about it." She looked up with tortured eyes. "Now you know the truth about me, don't you?"

"Anybody can make a mistake," he said.

"Not me."

"Why not you?"

"I'm not supposed to make mistakes. At least that's what I thought. And now all I do is mess up. And the thing is, I don't even know how I got to be this way. Excuse me, I've got a headache. I need to take something for it." She stood up to leave. "I am sorry about what I did."

"I know you are."

She took a couple of aspirin, then went back to Sarah's room and sprawled across her bed and wouldn't answer when Sarah asked what was wrong.

She fell asleep. When she woke up, it was eleven at night. But then she couldn't get back to sleep. Finally, at two in the morning, she got up and went into the living room. Except for the night-light in the bathroom, the house was dark.

She knelt down in front of the couch and rested her forehead against one of the cushions. It had been a long time since she'd talked to Heavenly Father. She had said prayers in church and in her family, but this was different. In this prayer she told him what she had done and how badly she felt about it now. And she explained how her mother thought she needed to go before the entire school and admit what she'd done. But most of all, she quit trying to hide what she had done.

As she was praying she felt a glimmer of hope, and a phrase from seminary popped into her mind. *I will not leave you comfortless.*

It kept ringing in her mind like a clear bell on a cold day. She knew who'd said it; this was the first time she needed the peace it had to offer.

The next day was Friday. There was a pep rally scheduled at school late in the day. The basketball team had a game Saturday night against their biggest rival. Classes had been dismissed early and the gym was packed. Wearing white shirts and black slacks, the pep band played the school fight song to fire everybody up before the rally started. Then the cheerleaders did a few cheers to get the crowd going. The students were in a good mood. It was the last day of school for two weeks.

Before the principal officially began the rally, he made a few announcements and then said, "Brittany Spaulding has asked to say a few words before I turn the time over to Coach Hill. Brittany?"

Brittany made her way to the microphone. She looked around the packed gym and cleared her throat. *I might not have any friends after this,* she thought.

"This is really hard." She stopped talking and looked over the crowd. Julia, Diane, and Amanda were sitting together on the second row of the bleachers. *They might not ever talk to me again*, she thought.

There was nothing to do but get it over with. She cleared her throat again. "I've done something really bad."

"All right, Brittany!" a troublemaker from the crowd called out. Everyone began to laugh. The rowdier boys started chanting, "Brittany, Brittany, Brittany . . . "

She changed the mood of the crowd with what she had to say next. "I was the one who started all the bad things people are saying about my cousin Ryan. I said that he had killed somebody in a fight and that's why he had to come here. None of that is true. Ryan's not like that at all. So all the bad things you've heard about him, they just aren't true. I know what I did was wrong. I've already talked to Ryan about it, but I knew I had to tell all of you, so you'd know the truth. Ryan is really a nice guy. If you have to be mean to somebody—if you have to make fun of some-body—do it to me, because Ryan hasn't done anything wrong. I'm really sorry for what I did."

She looked directly at Diane in the crowd, and tried to keep the tears from overwhelming her. "Diane . . . I'm really sorry . . . "

She was finished. She knew she couldn't stay in the gym. She had to get away. She walked to the doors leading to the hall, but once she was out of the gym she ran full speed to her locker. She had to do her combination twice because tears clouded her vision. She put on her coat and shut her locker.

The pep rally had started. She could hear the crowd chanting as the cheerleaders led them in the same cheers they had done when she was a freshman. The same cheers but for different people.

She wasn't sure if this was even her school anymore. Maybe she'd have to transfer to another school. *Just like Ryan,* she thought. *Now I know how he felt coming here.*

She saw Diane coming down the hall toward her. Brittany turned to run.

"Please don't run away!" Diane called out.

"I can't talk to you now. Give me some time to settle down," Brittany said.

"When?"

"Tonight, at the ward Christmas party."

"Okay."

"I've got to go now," Brittany said before turning and walking away.

It was cold, but Brittany walked home by herself. Her mother was gone, but she'd left a note: "Gone to get Sarah. Be back soon. I'll talk to you as soon as I get home to find out how things went. Love, Mom."

On her way to the room she and Sarah shared, she noticed a hand-lettered sign on Ryan's room that read, "Brittany's Room." It was written in Ryan's barely readable scrawl. She went to the door and opened it. All her pictures were back on the wall. She went to her closet. Ryan's clothes were gone but hers were there.

She went through the house trying to find where Ryan had put his things but couldn't find them anywhere. Finally, she went downstairs. Their basement was unfinished. All there had ever been down there was the furnace and some shelves her dad had made for food storage. She made her way down the rough wooden stairs. There, at the bottom, she saw a bed in the corner. A six-foot length of wire was stretched between two of the two-by-eights that supported the floor above. Ryan's clothes were hanging from the wire. Cardboard boxes were positioned on each side of his bed to hold his alarm clock, some books, and a lamp. A poster of

Michael Jordan had been taped to the bare cement wall. One of the top corners had come undone and was bent over, threatening to pull the poster clear off the wall.

She heard a car pull into the garage and a minute later a door opened. She could hear her mother and Sarah talking. And then steps as her mother came down the stairs.

"I see you've discovered what Ryan did. It was his idea. He came home after his first period class and helped me move everything. He wants you to have your room back."

"I told the whole school what I'd done."

"How did it go?" her mother asked.

"It was awful."

"But you did it?"

"Yes, I did it."

"Oh, Brittany, that must have been so hard." Her mother came to her, and they hugged each other.

That night at the ward Christmas party, some observers watching the nativity scene may have wondered why Mary seemed so emotional as she and Joseph tried to get a room at the inn. And why Julia, Diane, and Amanda came up afterward and threw their arms around the girl who played Mary. And why they were all so emotional about a simple nativity scene.

Brittany had learned the importance of having a place to come home to. Not an actual room, though, because she stayed only a few more months in her room before she went off to college. But she had found a place she could always go to. She had discovered that the son of Mary would be there for her when she needed comfort and peace and hope, that she could go to him and receive forgiveness for her mistakes and then go on with her life.

Brittany had found a place for Him in her heart.

HAVE YOURSELF A METAMORPHIC CHRISTMAS

On December 14, one day after Zach turned sixteen, his father reminded him that his mission was only three years away and that, so far, he had saved very little money for it. And so, after school the next day, Zach found an ad in the paper for a part-time job in sales over Christmas. He called the number and talked to Max Belken, the sales rep for Kitchen Miracle food processors. "So, tell me about yourself," Max said. His voice was low and gravelly, and he spoke with a blunt Eastern accent.

"Well, I'm a sophomore in high school." Zach wished there were more to say. "Oh, and I'm an Eagle Scout."

"An Eagle Scout, you say? You just might be what I'm looking for. I'll need to see you, though. Our temporary offices are at the Buena Vista Motel. Can you come now?"

"Yeah, sure."

"Good. When you get here, go to the desk and have 'em call me."

Fifteen minutes later Zach had his mother drop him off. He told her he'd walk home.

When Max Belken entered the motel lobby, he looked as though he hadn't had a full night's sleep for thirty years. He wore a dingy white shirt and a thin gray tie; the knot of

161

his tie was pulled away from his fleshy neck. He held a cigar in his short thick fingers.

Max conducted the interview in the lobby, sitting on a gaudy, reddish orange, vinyl-covered couch. Rips in the plastic had been mended with gray tape. Smoke from Max's cigar hung in the air like a stale curtain. "What the world needs now is a Kitchen Miracle in every home, and that's what we're trying to do here in . . . in . . . uh . . . don't tell me . . . " He took a big puff on his cigar and then started coughing. "Grand Rapids, right?"

Zach wondered how long Max had been on the road.

When Belken talked, his words came in sudden bursts like a machine gun, punctuated by jabs into the air with his cigar. "You look like a nice kid, so let me tell you what I'm looking for. I need somebody who can work alongside a real dish. You think you can do that?"

Zach wasn't sure what it meant to work alongside a dish. "Well, yeah, I guess so."

"Don't be so sure. This girl is dynamite. Her name's Ashley. The thing I'm concerned about, Kid, is I don't want you falling to pieces over her. That's what others have done in—let me see—Cleveland, Denver, Chicago, Detroit."

"I really don't think I'd have any trouble."

"Pretty sure of yourself aren't you? I like that. Just like me when I was your age. That's what got me to where I am today."

Zach glanced around and decided it wasn't such a great recommendation.

"So, are you interested or not?" Max asked.

"Yes, sir, I am."

"Good. Let's get down to business then." Max quickly ran through all the details of the job. When he was done, he asked, "You want to start now?"

"Sure, why not?"

"Let's go then."

Max Belken drove a large, enclosed, delivery-type van with Illinois license plates. "I'm going to give you three rules to follow, Kid," he said as they headed for the mall. "Rule Number One: Don't get in Ashley's way. She's a genius at keeping the product moving. Rule Number Two: You're Ashley's backup. It's like being in a play. She's the star; you're the one backstage making it happen. You prepare the potatoes and carrots Ashley uses in her demonstrations. You take the money. You make the change. You do the gift wrapping if they ask for it, but make sure they know it's a dollar extra. Rule Number Three: Stay with Ashley at all times. Do you understand what I'm saying? If we let her go to lunch with some guy, she might be gone an hour, maybe two. Don't get me wrong—I don't blame her for wanting to get away once in a while. But answer me this—when she goes off like that, what's happening to the product?"

"Nothing."

"Right. No offense, Kid, but nobody's going to buy a twenty-dollar potato peeler from either you or me. If Ashley's gone, the product doesn't move. And in back of this rig I got a truckload of product just waiting to be sold. If we don't move product, we're in deep, serious trouble."

"Yes, sir."

"Let me tell you something else. Without Ashley, what have we got? I'll tell you what we've got. We've got a potato peeler. And everybody's already got a potato peeler. Not only that, but how many people you know ever bought their wife a potato peeler for Christmas?"

"Not very many."

"Right. People don't buy potato peelers for Christmas. But with Ashley, they do. You want to know why I hired you? Because you're an Eagle Scout, and that's what I need around Ashley. So don't start taking a liking to her. She's too old for you. For that matter she's too . . . she's too everything for you. So keep being a Boy Scout, Kid. And whatever you do, don't turn out like the one I just fired." He shook his head. "That was a sad case, let me tell you."

"What happened?"

"We came here just after Thanksgiving. I hired a local guy to work with Ashley. But the idiot fell for her. He knew better too. I warned him about it from the beginning. Just like I'm warning you. She humored him along for a while and then, when things were getting out of hand, she told me he was getting in the way of her moving product. Well, that did it. I fired him on the spot and told him never to come back. But he did, after I'd gone. He made a big scene in front of everybody during a sales presentation. Somebody called the police and they took him away. For all I know, he's still in jail.

Let me tell you something, Kid. Ashley takes no prisoners, either at work or outside of work. Wherever she's at, she fits in, makes friends, gets along, but she forgets 'em all the minute we leave town. I don't know why she's that way, but she is. I've had her selling for me for over a year, and if she keeps at it, she's going to make both of us rich someday. That girl can move product. That's why I care about her like she was one of my own. But even so, I know that, deep inside, she's a machine. Now when you first meet her, you're going to think I've been too harsh on her, but, believe me, I haven't. Trust me."

He paused and then blew a puff of his cigar smoke in Zach's direction. "You want to know what Christmas means to me?" Max asked.

"I guess so."

"Christmas is the time of the year to move product." They pulled up in front of the mall. "I need to check on a few things, but I'll be back in a few minutes. In the meantime go in and introduce yourself to Ashley. Tell her you're the new man. The Kitchen Miracle booth is across from Musicland."

Zach phoned home to tell his mom he'd taken the job and would call her when he needed a ride home.

As he approached the Kitchen Miracle booth and spotted Ashley for the first time, he realized why Max Belken had warned him. She was the most beautiful girl he'd ever seen.

Zach liked to know the reason for everything. His mother said he got that from his dad, who was a geology professor at the college. At that moment Zach wanted to know what gave Ashley the advantage. Plenty of girls had long blonde hair; hers was darker, almost carmel-colored, and thicker than most. Other girls had green eyes, so that couldn't be it. There were girls in his school who were as tall, and a few even moved with the same dancer's grace she demonstrated. He watched her work and listened to her. She had an animated voice that she used to play the crowd like a musical instrument.

He moved forward and studied the men gathered around her as she did her demonstration. They responded to every joke and every move she made. The way she smiled and moved her hands was fascinating, and the men watched her intently, as if it were the first time they'd ever seen anyone peel a potato.

Zach waited until she finished her presentation and sold several of the Kitchen Miracle products. When she was alone, Zach approached the booth. "I'm Zach Miller. Mr. Belken said for me to tell you I'm the new man."

She patted him on the head. "The new man? I don't think so—but, hey, don't give up, you'll get there."

Zach blushed. She was right. Compared to her, he was still a kid.

"What do you want me to do?" he asked.

"For now, just watch. I'm about to do another demonstration."

It didn't take long for Zach to see why Belken valued Ashley. She could draw a crowd just by clearing her throat in the microphone that was clipped to her shirt.

After the presentation, Zach tried to help out where he could.

Max Belken showed up and watched from a distance until the last customer left; then he came over to them. "How's he going to work out?" he asked Ashley.

"He'll be okay. You're getting 'em younger and younger each time, aren't you?"

"You know why that is."

"You can't blame me for the last one," Ashley said.

"That's what you always say. It doesn't really matter now, anyway. Just try and make this work."

Belken had Zach help him carry some product from the van to the booth and then he left again. For the rest of the day it was all Zach could do to keep up with her. She'd do one demonstration, sell ten or fifteen peelers, wait five minutes, and then start all over again. A little before ten that night, just before the mall closed, Zach helped Ashley clean up the booth and get ready for the next day.

"You did okay for your first day," she said.

"Thanks."

She dumped the potatoes and carrots used in the presentations into the garbage can they kept in the booth. "Did Max warn you about me?"

"I don't know. I guess so."

"What did he say?"

"He said you don't take prisoners. I'm not sure what that means."

"It means that the guys I work with end up liking me more than I like them."

"Oh. Is that bad?"

"For them it is. How you getting home?"

"I'll call my mom."

"I can take you."

"Okay. Thanks."

They left the mall and walked to her car. "Nice car," Zach said of the sporty compact.

"It's a rental. I hate being driven around in that old van Max drives, so when we're going to stay in a place for a while, I always rent my own car. Kitchen Miracle pays for half of it." She let him in. "What do you do for excitement in a town like this?" she asked.

"I play soccer for our school, but that's in the fall. I'm interested in geology too. My dad teaches it at the college. Last summer I went with him and some of his students on a one-month field trip. It was great. I'm thinking about becoming a geologist someday."

"You must like rocks then, right?"

"Yeah, I do."

"When I first saw you, I figured you were real smart."

"What will you do when you get back to your motel room?"

"Order something from room service and eat and maybe read a book."

"That doesn't sound too exciting."

"When I first started working for Max, I'd always end up in a bar after work. But after a while a person gets sick of that. Guys saying the same thing night after night. It's no good, Zach. When Max fired the guy you replaced, I decided that from now on I'm staying out of bars. So I bought a book. I'm going to read it, too."

They pulled into his driveway. "You want to come in?" Zach asked. "I could show you my rock collection. I worked on it all last summer with my dad. You want to see it?"

"Some other time, okay? I'd really like to, but I'm kind of wiped out tonight."

"I could bring a few rocks to work some day, if you're interested."

"Well, sure, Zach, why not? I might as well learn a few things from you while we're working together."

By Saturday Zach was doing his share of the work. Even Max was impressed when he came around to check up on them. "Keep it up, you two." After an hour of standing around Max left.

Zach and Ashley worked straight through until nearly three o'clock. "Zach, let's take a break. I've got to stop and eat or I'm going to pass out. All I've had all day is a bagel and some orange juice."

That morning, when Zach had come to work, he'd brought a tote bag with some rocks from his collection. He carried it with him when they went to eat. They ate in the food court of the mall. Ashley wanted Vietnamese fast food. Because Ashley recommended it, Zach ordered some for himself. He was surprised how much he liked it.

At first it was awkward being with her when they weren't working. He felt like he should bring up something interesting, but he couldn't think of anything to say. She tried to get things going by asking him about school.

"It's okay, I guess." He didn't like it when adults asked about school. They never really wanted to know anyway.

Zach didn't do much better. "How come you never went to college?" he asked.

Her eyes flashed. "Because I didn't have things handed to me like some people. I've had to work for everything I've ever got."

Right after that he spilled some sauce on his shirt. She helped him wipe it off. It made him feel like a little kid.

He decided he couldn't do much worse by bringing out his rock collection. He opened the tote bag and said, "I brought you some rocks to look at."

She picked up the rock he'd just set on the table. "Yep, that's a rock all right. No doubt about it."

Because looking at her distracted him, he focused his attention on the rock. "Basically, there are three kinds of rock."

She couldn't take this seriously. "Wait—don't tell me—let me guess . . . big rocks, little rocks, and pebbles. Right?"

"No. It's sedimentary, igneous, and metamorphic. We're doing sedimentary rock today."

"Zach, let me ask you a question—how old are you?"

"Sixteen."

"No kidding! You're way more organized than I was at your age." She paused. "Do you want to know how old I am?"

"I guess so."

"I'm twenty-three. If I'd lived around here when you were growing up, I could've been your baby-sitter. That's something to think about, isn't it?"

Just then an older-looking, handsome man passed by them. He smiled at her and then noticed the rocks on the table. Ashley turned to the man and gave him a big smile. "You got to respect anybody who brings a bag of rocks to lunch, right?"

The man returned her smile and continued on his way.

Zach didn't appreciate being made fun of. "I wouldn't have brought 'em to work, but you told me you wanted to learn about rocks."

"You're right. And I do, too. It's just that I've never known anybody like you before, that's all. It's great, though. Really. Just go ahead with your little lesson."

He didn't appreciate her calling it a little lesson but didn't say anything about it. He handed her a rock. "This is called shale. On the other side you can see a fossil."

She turned it over. "Zach, you're not going to test me on all this afterward, are you?" she asked with a teasing smile.

"Don't make fun of me," he said. He started to pack up the rocks.

"I wasn't making fun of you, Zach. Honest."

"I can't help the way I am."

"You're fine the way you are . . . really . . . I'm serious. You're one in a million, believe me. Show me some more rocks."

He reached into his tote bag again. "Okay, this is sandstone. Sandstone is not always soft, but this piece is. See, you can scratch it with your fingernail."

"I'm usually very particular about my fingernails. Well, all right, here goes . . . " She scratched the rock. "You're right. It scratches real easy."

A tall, good-looking man in his late twenties came over to talk to Ashley. "Excuse me, but is your first name Ashley?"

"Maybe. Who wants to know?"

"I'm Brandon Parker. I work at Musicland. Mind if I sit down?"

"We're about to leave," Ashley said.

"Ross Kellogg is a friend of mine. He asked me to say hello."

"Ross Kellogg?"

"Don't tell me you don't remember him. He remembers you—in a big way. When I first started working here, all he could talk about was last Christmas when he met you. He's not working here anymore, but I was thinking, maybe we could go out for a drink sometime."

Ashley glanced at Zach. "I don't hang out in bars like I used to."

"Well, it doesn't have to be that. We can do anything you want. I'm pretty sure you'll have more fun with me than with your little friend here."

"Zach and I work together. Look, can't you take a hint?"

"I'm going, but if you change your mind, you know where to find me. My name's in the phone book too."

After the man walked away, Zach mimicked, "My name's in the phone book—in the yellow pages—under scumbags."

"Sorry," Ashley said.

"You spend time with guys like him?" Zach asked.

"I used to, but not anymore. You know what, Zach? I wish I'd had a friend like you when I was your age."

"What kind of friends did you have?"

"Mostly predators." She picked up the sandstone, held it in one hand and gently scratched it with her fingernail. She watched as the grains of sand fell on the tabletop.

"It doesn't take much to break it apart," Zach said.

"No, it doesn't. It doesn't take much at all." Her face clouded over, and she stared at the rock.

"Is something wrong?" he asked.

She looked over at him and smiled. "No, everything's

fine. Just feeling sorry for myself, that's all. But I'm okay now. Let's get back."

On their way to the booth, he said, "Monday is my first day of Christmas vacation, so I'll be working full time from now on."

"That's great, Zach. I can always use the help."

"On Monday, if you want, we could do igneous."

"Yeah, sure, whatever you say."

On Monday Zach brought some samples of igneous rock, but they were too busy until closing time to talk. He wasn't going to say anything about it, but as they were getting ready to leave the mall, she noticed him carrying the bag. "You got some more rocks to show me, Zach?"

"Yeah, a few."

"Well, let's take a look at 'em."

They sat on a bench inside the mall. "Okay, today we're doing igneous rock," Zach said. "Mostly they come from volcanoes. This one is called basalt. Careful, it's kind of heavy." He handed it to her.

"Where'd you get this?"

"My uncle sent it to me from Idaho."

"No kidding. Max and I worked a mall in Boise once."

"This is pumice. It's so light it'll float in water." He handed it to her.

"Wow, that is light."

In the next few minutes he showed her four other kinds of rocks.

"Zach, let me ask you a question. If you were a rock, what kind of a rock would you be?"

"I don't know."

"I think you'd be sedimentary," she said.

"Why?" he asked.

"Because you take in information all the time."

"What kind would you be?" he asked.

"Igneous, I guess."

"How come?"

"Because igneous rocks come from fire and heat. That pretty much describes me."

Suddenly, out of nowhere, Max showed up, looking mad. "What's going on? Why isn't the booth still open?"

"Look at the clock, Max," Ashley snapped. "It's almost ten."

"How come I see stores that are still open?"

Ashley stood up to face Max. She towered over him. "What's the deal here? Now we have to be the very last one to close up? I work hard all day. If you want us to stay open until everybody else has gone home, then how about if you come here and help out? As far as I can tell, you're the most under-worked part of this team. What do you do all day, anyway?"

"What do you think I do? I do paperwork. There's a lot more to this business than you think there is. And another thing, I thought I warned you to stay away from the kid. I won't have you messing him up like you've done with all the others."

She held up her hand to stop him. "That's it, I quit."

"What are you talking about?"

"You heard me—I don't have to take this from you. Find some other fool you can get to do all the work. Let's go, Zach. I'll take you home, and then I'm leaving for good."

Once they were outside, it was a race—Ashley in the lead, Zach following close behind, and Max falling farther behind with each step, desperately trying to make up the distance with his voice. "You think I can't get along without you? Well, you're wrong!"

Ashley turned around and walked backwards. "Do it then, because I'm out of here."

"You can't make it without me," Max called out. "Who's going to bail you out when you get thrown in jail for DUI?"

"That happened one time, Max. I'm not like that anymore."

"I don't believe that. You'll always be the same."

They were now in the outer reaches of the parking lot. Zach wished he wasn't there. He wasn't used to people yelling at one another at the top of their voices in the middle of a parking lot.

Max's wheezing became worse with each step. "Wait up," he finally called out.

She stopped walking and waited for him to catch up.

"There's no reason for us to split up now when things are going so well," he said between labored gasps of air.

"I can't work for someone who doesn't respect me," she said.

"I respect you."

"You don't respect me as a person. You think just because I've made a few mistakes that I'm always going to be messing up. But that's not necessarily true. And as for Zach—he's just teaching me about rocks."

"Rocks? Are you crazy? Why would anybody want to know about rocks?"

"Rocks are interesting, Max. Really. There's your sedimentary rocks and then there's your igneous rocks. Isn't that right, Zach?"

"That's right."

Ashley spoke quietly to Zach. "He'll never apologize. He can't ever admit it when he's wrong."

"How come?" Zach asked.

"I don't know. Some men are like that."

"You know a lot about men, don't you?" he said.

"Don't you start on me, too," she warned.

"I didn't mean anything by it."

Max cleared his throat. "How early did you close up?" This time it was not a demand.

"About ten minutes. The reason we shut down is that we ran out of product, Max. We sold all you brought us this morning."

Max couldn't believe it. "All of it?"

"All but one. Max, you want us to give you a lift back to the van?"

When Max got out of her car once they reached his van, his pride forced him to unleash at least one parting shot. "You know, you might have sold the last one if you'd stayed open ten more minutes."

"Maybe so, Max. Maybe so. I'll see you tomorrow."

Zach was confused. One minute Max and Ashley were yelling at each other, and she was quitting. Now she was saying she'd see him tomorrow. *They must do this all the time,* he thought.

They were so busy the next few days that Zach didn't get a chance to show Ashley his samples of metamorphic rocks. Finally, on Thursday night, they looked at them after work while sitting in a Burger King across the street from the mall.

When they pulled into the parking lot, Ashley turned on the dash light and put new lipstick on and checked her makeup. Zach was glad she felt comfortable enough around him to do that. It was as if he had been allowed into some private part of her life.

She turned to him when she was finished. "Well, what do you think?"

He wanted to tell her how much he liked to look at

her face, but he knew that would ruin everything. "It's okay, I guess."

Inside, when it was time to pay for what they'd ordered, Zach offered to pay, but she wouldn't let him and ended up paying for it all. While they ate, Zach pulled out the rocks he'd brought from home. "Okay, the last kind of rock is metamorphic. They used to be igneous or sedimentary, but either pressure or heat from the earth changed them into something else." He handed her a caramel-colored rock. "This is marble."

"This is beautiful," she said.

"Yeah, I know. It's my favorite."

"What did this used to be?"

"Limestone."

"Do the metamorphics always end up better off than they were?"

"Some do, like marble. They make statues out of marble, you know."

"This would make a wonderful statue." She turned the piece of marble over in her hand. "So, for this rock, all the pressure and the heat turned out to be a good thing."

"I guess so."

"So even rocks can change, right?"

"Sure, and they do it all the time, too. Not only that, but the whole earth is always re-creating itself. There are places in the bottom of the ocean where lava is coming up and making new ocean floor. And near the Hawaiian Islands there's a hot spot where lava comes spewing out and makes one island after another. And when an island is first made, it's basalt like I showed you before. And then one day a bird lands on it, and maybe the bird brings with it some seeds from something it's eaten, and the seed ends up on the black basalt, and it starts to grow, and that brings more birds, and pretty soon you have Oahu Island.

But it all started with molten rock that got hard, like this basalt. So you can never tell what's going to happen." Zach was excited and was speaking rapidly.

She picked up the piece of marble again and turned it over in her hand. "No kidding. That's really interesting, Zach."

Usually, when she took him home, she had a music tape playing, but that night she didn't turn it on. "Zach, let me ask you a question. If the earth can start over, shouldn't a person be able to?"

"Yeah, sure."

"You think so? Sometimes people can start out okay but then something bad happens and they get into a pattern and they can't seem to get out of it."

"Did that happen to you?"

She sighed. "Yeah, pretty much."

"I'm sorry."

"Me too. I want to be like that piece of marble you showed me and change into something better. I don't want to be living out of a suitcase for the rest of my life. Someday I'm going to quit this job and go off to college and get an education. And someday I want to have a real house with maybe an apple tree. And be married to a guy who treats me good. You think that's asking too much?"

"No." They pulled into his driveway. "Come and talk to my folks."

"Why?"

"They might be able to help you. They know a lot about life."

"Maybe some other time, Zach, okay? I'm kind of tired tonight."

"Yeah, sure." It was time for him to leave, and he wanted her to know he valued her friendship, but he didn't know what to say. In what was his first attempt ever to show affection for a girl, he reached over and placed his hand on her forearm and patted it a couple of times. She looked over at him and smiled. It was so unlike him to touch anyone that he started to blush. He didn't want her to see how red his face was, so he muttered a quick good-bye and hurried out of the car.

When he got inside the house, his parents were waiting for him. "Zach, where have you been?" his mother asked. "It's after eleven. The mall closes at ten. What took you so long to get home?"

"Nothing."

"I had a phone call today from a friend of mine who works at the mall," his mother said. "She said that you're spending a lot of time with that girl you work with."

Zach shrugged his shoulders. "We work together, that's all."

"The person who called said it looked like more than that to her. Zach, she's way too old for you."

"I know that. All we do is work together."

"You were with her tonight after work though, weren't you?" his dad asked.

"Yes, but that was just because we were both hungry. We went to Burger King. I showed her some of my rocks. I don't see why you're making such a big deal out of this."

"We're worried you might be getting into something you're not ready for," his dad said.

"She's not exactly your girl next door," his mother said.

"You're taking someone else's word for all this?" Zach asked.

His mother hesitated. "Well, not really. After I got the phone call, I went out to the mall. I had to see for myself what she is like."

"You spied on us?" Zach said.

"You're my son. I have to watch out for your best interest."

"So what did you see?" Zach asked.

"I saw a young woman who's much too old for you."

"We're just friends. What's wrong with that?"

"Nothing, but at the same time," his mother said, "I don't think she's the kind of person you should be spending time with after work."

"Tonight she said she wants to change the way she's been living."

"Fine, let her change all she wants," his mother said. "I just don't want her changing my son. From now on, we'll pick you up after work."

"No! Just stay out of this!" He went to his room and slammed the door, changed into his sweats, and left the house. He ran as hard as he could until his lungs ached. He felt guilty for raising his voice, but his parents couldn't treat him like a child.

By the time he arrived back home, he had calmed down. When he entered the house, his parents were still sitting at the kitchen table.

"Zach, while you've been gone your mother and I have had a chance to talk," his father said. "If you want to talk to this girl after work about your rock collection or about how she can change her life, fine, go ahead—but bring her home with you. We'd like to be her friends too."

Zach thought about it for a minute and then said, "Okay."

The next day at work things were so busy that he and Ashley didn't have any time at all to talk. As she drove him home after work, she complained about having a headache, so Zach didn't ask her to come in with him to meet his parents.

On December 23 there was a heavy snowstorm that

kept shoppers from going to the mall. Zach and Ashley took a break at one-thirty for lunch.

"My mom and dad would like you to come in and meet them when you take me home tonight."

"Sure, Zach, that sounds good. I'd like to tell them what a great son they've got."

"So tonight is okay for you?" he asked.

"Yeah, sure."

While they were eating, Brandon from Musicland came over to their table. "Not too crowded today, is it?" he asked.

"Not really," Ashley said. "A nice break from the way it's been."

"Well, enjoy it because they'll be back tomorrow."

To Zach it seemed that Brandon was trying hard not to be a jerk.

"Mind if I sit down?" Brandon asked.

"I guess not," she said.

Brandon sat down. "So what have you been doing lately?"

"Not much," Ashley said.

"I was wondering if you'd care to have something to eat with me after work tonight," Brandon said.

"She's going home with me after work," Zach said.

"Why?"

"My parents want to meet her."

Brandon smiled at Ashley. "Sounds pretty serious."

"It doesn't have to be tonight, does it, Zach?" Ashley asked.

"My mom said she was going to make a cake and everything."

"I know, but how about tomorrow after work? We'll be closing early. Maybe I could meet your parents then."

Zach knew what this was all about. "You're going to end up in some bar with him, aren't you?"

"We won't end up at a bar, but even if we did, we are adults," she said.

"But you told me you didn't want to do that anymore."

"I can't stay my entire life in a motel room reading a book. I have to get out once in a while."

"Fine then," Zach muttered. "Do whatever you want. I don't care."

"You know what?" Brandon said, "I think young Zach here has a crush on you."

"Why don't you just shut your mouth up?" Zach stormed away. He went back to the Kitchen Miracle booth and cleaned with a fury.

She came back ten minutes later. "You cleaned up, didn't you? It looks good. Thanks, Zach."

"You're going to see him tonight, aren't you?" he asked.

"No, Zach. I'm going home with you to meet your mom and dad."

He couldn't believe it. "Really?"

"Really."

That night after work, when they pulled into his parents' driveway, Ashley said, "Tomorrow's Christmas Eve, Zach, and it'll be really busy, especially because of the storm today. I want to get plenty of sleep tonight, so I probably won't stay very long."

"That's okay."

He got through the introductions all right and then they sat down and talked and had cake and ice cream. Zach found it all very awkward. At work Ashley treated him as if they were the same age, but around his parents she was the adult who worked with their son.

Zach wanted his parents to tell Ashley how she could

make changes in her life. After ten minutes, though, it didn't seem like it was ever going to come up. Zach decided to force it. "Ashley used to spend a lot of time in bars with a bunch of losers, but she's trying to stop all that now. I told her you'd be able to tell her how to do it."

From everyone's reaction, he knew it was the wrong thing to say.

Ashley's face hardened. "Well, I guess you know all my secrets now. I don't want you to think I'm a really bad person. It's just that I never know anybody when I'm in a new town, and I hate to stay in my room all the time, so sometimes I like to get out and meet a few people."

"Of course," Zach's mother said a little too quickly. "That's fine."

"It isn't fine," Zach said. "You should see the kind of guys who go after her. The one hanging on her now is a real slimeball."

"Zach is always looking out for me," Ashley said with an iron smile. "I'd better be going. We have a big day tomorrow. Our last day, Zach. I'll miss having you teach me all about rocks."

A few polite good-byes and then she escaped. Zach felt devastated. "Why didn't you tell her what she needs to do to change?" he asked his father.

"I heard you saying that's what she wanted, but I didn't hear her say it."

"She told me before."

"Sometimes it's hard for people to turn their lives around, Zach," his mother said.

"You don't think she can, do you?" Zach said.

"I didn't say that."

"No, but I can tell. You don't think she'll ever change."

"Is this about her changing, or is this about something else?" his dad asked.

"What do you mean?"

"What are your feelings for her?" his mother asked.

Zach didn't answer right away. "She's my friend. I want her to . . . I want her to take the missionary lessons and join the Church and start going to college."

"Maybe she doesn't want to change that much," his mother said.

"No, she does."

"Why not give her a copy of the Book of Mormon, Zach?" his dad suggested. "Joseph Smith said a person can get closer to God by abiding by its precepts than through any other book. You could write your testimony in the book and then give it to her tomorrow. I'm pretty sure she'd accept it from you."

His dad helped him locate a blue, soft-cover copy of the Book of Mormon in a bookshelf, and then his parents went to bed. Zach sat at the kitchen table and worked on what he'd write on the inside cover. He wanted it to be just right, so he wrote it over and over on scratch paper until he got it just the way he wanted it. It was after eleven o'clock, when he finally finished, but he was so excited, he knew he wouldn't be able to sleep. He wondered if Ashley was asleep. Probably not. She was probably reading in her room. If he got the book to her that night, she might have time to read a little of it before work the next day.

He went into his parents' bedroom. His folks were asleep. "Dad?" he said softly.

"What?"

"Can I talk to you?"

His father listened as Zach asked for a ride to Ashley's motel so he could give her a copy of the Book of Mormon. Then he got out of bed and got dressed.

"You're not really going to take him over there at this time of night, are you?" his mother asked.

"It's not that late for someone Ashley's age," his dad said.

While waiting for his dad to get dressed, Zach went to the kitchen and picked up the sheets of scratch paper he'd used to practice what he finally wrote in her book. He put them on top of his desk in his room. He also grabbed the piece of marble from his rock collection, the one Ashley liked so much. He would give that to her also.

When they pulled up in front of the motel, his dad asked, "Do you want me to come in, Zach?"

"Not really."

"I'll wait here, then."

Zach's plan was to go to the desk and get Ashley's room number, but when he entered the lobby, he passed the motel bar. He looked in and saw Ashley sitting at a table with Brandon.

Zach stood in the doorway and watched the two of them. There were drinks in front of them and they were talking.

Zach watched them for a long time. At one point Brandon put his hand on her knee. It was just for a second, more of a way to emphasize a point than anything else, but to Zach it was wrong.

When Ashley turned to look at the clock, she saw Zach standing in the doorway. She excused herself and came out into the lobby. "Zach, what are you doing here?"

"Why are you with him in a bar?" he asked.

"Zach, I'm over twenty-one. I can be here if I want. We're just having a drink, that's all. And then I'm sending him home."

"That's what you say now, but if you keep drinking, who knows what will happen?"

"Nothing is going to happen."

"You let him put his hand on your knee."

"I'm a big girl now, Zach. I can take care of myself. Why did you come here?"

"I came to give you something, but I'm not sure if I should now."

"It's up to you, Zach, but you can't stay here, that's for sure. You're not old enough."

"If I was older, would you let me spend time with you like he's doing?"

She spoke almost wistfully. "Zach . . . you're a wonderful boy, and everything, but I think that if you were my age, you probably wouldn't want to spend time with me."

"No, you're wrong. It wouldn't make any difference." He decided to go ahead with his plans. He handed her the piece of marble and the book. "I guess this is my Christmas present for you. Sorry I didn't wrap it like I should've."

"This is real nice, Zach. Thank you very much."

"I did this because . . . " Not sure what else to say, he stammered, " . . . because I . . . because I want you to be happy."

"That is so sweet, Zach. I mean it."

He touched the cover of the book. "A person can get closer to God by reading this book than from any other book . . . " He stopped. It seemed out of place to be saying something like that just outside a bar. "Will you read it?"

"I will, Zach. I promise. Do you need a ride home?"

"No, my dad is waiting in the car."

Carrying his drink in his hand, Brandon got up and walked toward them. "Kind of late for you, isn't it, Zach? A boy like you needs his sleep."

Zach didn't even acknowledge Brandon. He looked

directly at Ashley. "I'll see you tomorrow," he said and then walked away.

After Zach got back to the car, his father asked, "Did you give it to her?"

"Yeah, but she was in the bar with that same jerk."

The next morning at the Kitchen Miracle booth it was awkward for him to be around Ashley. They hardly spoke to each other at first, except for her asking him to go buy some carrots and potatoes for her presentations.

When he returned from the store, Ashley handed him the piece of marble he had given her the night before. "Zach, here, you'd better keep this. I'm sorry it smells so bad. After you left, Brandon dropped it in his drink. He called it 'whiskey on the rocks.' That's when I told him to leave. I let it soak in water all night, but it still smells. I'm really sorry."

"It doesn't matter now, anyway," Zach said, tossing the piece of marble into the garbage can.

"Zach . . ."

"What?"

"Listen to me—you were hoping for too much. Did you really think I was going to turn my life around all at once? That'd be the biggest miracle in the world."

"It would have happened if you'd just given it a chance."

"Sorry to disappoint you, but it's my life, and I'm the one who has to live it—not you."

The mall was scheduled to close at four o'clock. At three-thirty, Max came and announced they might as well start packing up. Zach helped Max carry the parts of the booth to the Kitchen Miracle van while Ashley went to Musicland to say good-bye to Brandon.

In half an hour Max and Zach were through loading the van. Max paid him and said that if they ever got back to the area, they'd call him to see if he wanted to work for them again.

"Don't bother," Zach said.

"She got to you, didn't she?" Max said.

It was painful for Zach to admit. "I guess she did."

"I tried to warn you, Kid."

"I know. I should have listened."

"You'll remember her, but she won't remember you. She never does."

"So nothing ever changes, does it?" Zach said.

"Not really. Well, anyway, good job, Kid." Max shook his hand.

Zach needed time to think, so he walked home.

Max went back inside the mall. Ashley was waiting for him. All that remained of the Kitchen Miracle booth was the garbage can. "I'll empty that and then we can be on our way," Max said to Ashley.

"Wait a minute," she said. She rummaged through the discarded potatoes and carrots and found the piece of marble Zach had given her.

"What's that?" Max asked.

"Just a souvenir."

"Whatever. Let's get going. We'll take a few weeks off and then get geared up for Valentine's Day in Denver."

Max emptied the garbage can into one of the dull grey receptacles scattered throughout the mall and then they both walked out to the van and got in. As they were driving away, Ashley placed the Book of Mormon Zach had given her under the seat. She set the piece of marble on the dashboard of the van.

"So, what's so important about that rock?"

"You really want to know?"

"I asked, didn't I?"

"All right. Well, this is marble. It's metamorphic. It

used to be something else, but it got changed into something better."

"What made it change?" Max asked.

She thought about it. "Life made it change."

"Did Zach give it to you?"

She told him how it ended up in the trash can.

"I can't believe this. What are you saying, that the kid got to you?"

"Don't call him the kid. His name is Zach. And, yes, he got to me—a little."

"How come? He was just a kid."

"He believed in me, Max. He's about the only one who ever has."

"I believe in you."

"All you really care about me is that I can sell. Zach taught me what life is all about."

"And what's that?"

"It's about change."

"I don't see you doing much in that department."

"It takes time. Did you know the Hawaiian Islands used to be a pile of black rock from a volcano? And now look at them. So never say somebody's not going to change. Sometimes it takes years. I'll do it, too, someday. You'll see. Someday I won't be spending my time in a bar with some guy I don't even like that much. Someday I'll go to college and learn all about rocks or whatever else I can think of."

"I'll believe it when I see it," he said. "You really think you'll remember him?"

"I do, Max."

"Well, that'll be a first."

She picked up the rounded, smooth piece of marble and rubbed it with her hands. "Merry Christmas, Max."

He seemed a little surprised. He looked over at her. "Merry Christmas, Girl."

They drove through the night until they reached Chicago on Christmas morning. It was a cold, gray morning, but the sun came out later in the day.

*   *   *

After Zach opened presents with his family, and after their traditional breakfast of tangerines, sweet rolls, and hot chocolate, Zach went to his room and closed the door, and from the scraps of scratch paper he'd used in coming up with a final draft, he read again what he'd written in Ashley's Book of Mormon.

Dear Ashley, The piece of marble I'm giving you with this book used to be just some common, everyday limestone. And now look at it! I think that you're like that too, and some day you'll turn into the kind of person you really want to be. This book will help you get there if you'll let it. Please read it and then ask God if it's true. He'll let you know that it is! And if you ever get discouraged, just remember that marble comes from limestone!

Zach's father found him in his room. "You okay?"

"She's never going to change, is she?" Zach said.

"You can never say that."

"She won't though, I'm pretty sure."

"People do change, though. Mary Magdalene changed. When the Savior first met her, she must've been in a bad way, because He cast seven devils from her. She was never the same after that. In fact, she was the first person Christ appeared to after his resurrection. That was a great honor for her, to be the first to see Him. She changed because of the Savior, and Ashley might change too, for the same reason. You never know."

*   *   *

It was not until the first of February, on their way to Denver for Valentine's Day, that Ashley noticed the copy of the Book of Mormon she'd stuck under the seat of the van on Christmas Eve. She picked it up and began to thumb through it.

"What's that?" Max asked.

"It's the book Zach gave me. I'd forgotten that I put it under the seat."

"Zach who?"

"You know, from Christmas. The one with the rocks."

"Rocks in his head, if you ask me," Max muttered.

"You want me to read this to you?"

"I got better things to do with my time."

"Right, sure you do, Max."

Ashley first read what Zach had written in the book, and then she turned to page one and began to read.

QUORUM LESSON NUMBER ONE

After sacrament meeting, Bishop Merrill told Kirk and Jonathan he wanted to talk to them following his scheduled interviews. Kirk knew it was because the bishop had seen them talking at the sacrament table during the opening hymn and the first part of the meeting.

Being called into the bishop's office was just one more reason for Kirk to wish he'd never left Idaho. His family had moved to Nebraska in July, just before his junior year. He went from a ward with twenty-three priests to a new ward with only one other active priest, Jonathan Davenport. Kirk had nothing in common with Jonathan. Kirk liked sports and outdoor activities while Jonathan was in the high school orchestra and was writing a Broadway musical.

Bishop Merrill was not at all like his bishop back in Idaho, who loved the outdoors and often went with the boys on their overnight camping trips. Bishop Merrill was a small man, about five-foot-eight, with rounded shoulders and with very little hair on top of his head. Kirk couldn't imagine Bishop Merrill climbing a mountain with a group of boys. Of course it wasn't a problem because Nebraska didn't have any real mountains, anyway.

When Kirk told his mother he had to stay after church

to talk to the bishop, she asked if Kirk wanted them to
wait for him. He said no. He didn't want her to know he
was in trouble.

By one o'clock Kirk and Jonathan were still waiting outside the bishop's office. "What's your favorite
Broadway musical?" Jonathan asked.

Kirk was in no mood to talk about Broadway musicals.
"I don't know."

"Well, you must have a favorite."

"Why do I have to have a favorite? Do you have a
favorite NFL team?"

"Not really. I don't like football."

"Fine—I don't like musicals."

"I bet you'd like *Phantom of the Opera*. I'll sing you some
songs from it."

Kirk endured hearing Jonathan sing one song after
another. *Why me?* he thought.

Finally Bishop Merrill finished his last interview and
asked Kirk and Jonathan to come into his office. Kirk
noticed the bishop looked tired.

"Thanks for waiting," the bishop said. "Do you know
why I wanted to talk to you both?"

Jonathan cracked first. "It's because Kirk was talking
to me at the sacrament table, isn't it?"

Fine, put all the blame on me, Kirk thought.

"Kirk, what were you talking about that was so important?" Bishop Merrill asked.

"I was telling Jonathan about the BYU football game."
Kirk was hoping that by mentioning BYU, it would make
it more acceptable.

"I see." The bishop said, removing his glasses and rub-
bing the bridge of his nose.

Kirk tried to head off a long lecture. "We won't do it
again, will we, Jonathan?"

"Not me. I wanted to sing the opening song, but you kept talking. I don't know why you were telling me, anyway, because I really don't like football that much."

"I know you don't, but you should," Kirk said. "If you'd pay a little more attention to football, maybe people would start calling you Jon."

"Why would I want them to call me Jon? I like being called Jonathan."

Kirk shook his head. There was nobody like Jonathan back in Idaho. He had a speaking voice that really irritated Kirk. And yet when he sang, he sounded like an opera star. So it was either feast or famine in the voice department. Also, Jonathan seemed to have no interest in developing his body. He didn't lift weights, he didn't run, he didn't even like to arm wrestle. What he did, though, was take singing lessons. That meant he had exercises. To Kirk it was nearly unbearable when Jonathan did vocal exercises in front of other people without even asking permission. One exercise especially annoyed Kirk. It was a yawning sound that began high and continued downward, like a siren in reverse, until the pitch got so low it sounded like the last groans from a dying man.

In class Jonathan showed agreement with the teacher by nodding his head up and down. Sometimes Kirk thought Jonathan looked like one of those toy dogs with a bobbing head that some people display in the back window of their car. Kirk's style was to act a little bored during a lesson.

The bishop reached for his scriptures. Jonathan must have also feared a long lecture. "Bishop, I have to practice for a song I'm going to do for sacrament meeting next week. I arranged with Sister Olsen that we'd practice at one-thirty. Do you want me to call and tell her I'll be a little late?"

"No, you go ahead, Jonathan. I'll talk to Kirk now."

For the first time in his life Kirk wished he'd learned to play a musical instrument. He watched with envy as Jonathan left. Now it was just him and the bishop. "You look tired, Bishop."

"Do I? Sorry."

"Do you want to do this another time?"

"No, let's do it now. It's not going to take long." He looked at his watch. "Maybe we could speed this up though. I have some scriptures I'd like you to read. If you can read them by next Sunday, maybe we could talk about them after church."

"All right. I can do that. Anything else?"

The bishop pulled a piece of paper from his desk drawer and began to write down the scriptures he wanted Kirk to read. When he finished writing, he looked up. "Kirk, I know you miss being in Idaho, but I can tell you this—we need you here."

"I never wanted to move here."

"I've sensed that."

"We had twenty-three priests in our quorum back home. My bishop really likes the outdoors. He loves to hike in the summer and go cross-country skiing in the winter. He used to take us out all the time. Just before we moved, he led all the priests to the top of the Grand Tetons." Kirk paused. "Have you ever done anything like that?"

The bishop smiled. "I get dizzy on a Ferris wheel."

"That's okay. Not everybody can do that, I guess."

"How do you and Jonathan get along?"

"Well, okay, I guess, on the surface, but I don't think we'll ever be good friends."

"If we're going to have a strong quorum . . . "

"I hate to be negative, but how can we have a strong quorum with just two people?"

"It can be done."

Kirk didn't believe him but decided not to say anything more about it.

"Kirk, there's something I'd like to share with you." Bishop Merrill paused. He seemed to be searching for words. Then he said, "I wish you could know what it's like for me to sit on the stand and look out on the congregation every Sunday. We've got some great ward members, but I also see people with problems. I'd like to help more, but there's only so much I can do. We have to look to the Savior for the best kind of help. That's why we need to remember Him in our meetings. We need the Spirit to heal and comfort those who are hurting. Anything that detracts from the Spirit takes away from the blessings our members should be receiving by being in that meeting."

The bishop stopped talking. He appeared to be deep in thought. Then he leaned forward and spoke confidentially. "Some of our ward members are working through some very difficult situations. Try to imagine something. Let's say there is a brother in the ward who has been disciplined by the stake president and has been asked not to partake of the sacrament for a while. He feels horrible about what he has done and has continued to attend and is working through his problems. It probably won't be very long until he is allowed to participate again. How do you suppose he'll feel about that ordinance when he is finally permitted to take the bread and water again?"

For the first time Kirk felt bad for having talked during the first part of sacrament meeting.

The bishop continued. "Do you understand that when you break the bread and when you repeat the sacrament prayers, you are standing in for the Savior? If he were with

us in the meeting, he very well might choose to administer
the sacrament to us. Since he can't be here, you represent
him. Today, when I looked over and saw you and Jonathan
sitting at the sacrament table carrying on a conversation,
it really bothered me. The two of you were about to participate in one of the most sacred ordinances in the
Church, but you were behaving as though it was no big
deal. I'm sorry to have to say so, but it was disappointing.
If we're going to succeed in what the Lord expects of us,
we're going to need your help."

Kirk felt he was being unfairly singled out. He saw
people talking during sacrament meeting all the time. Out
of respect for the bishop, though, he didn't try to argue
with him. Besides that, he was hungry and just wanted to
get home. "It won't happen again, Bishop."

"Thank you. Can I give you a ride home now?"

"Yeah, sure, that'd be great."

"I need to lock up the building on our way out,"
Bishop Merrill said as they left his office. "It sounds like
you really liked your bishop in Idaho. I've only been bishop
for about nine months. If you ever have any suggestions
about what I need to be doing with our youth, I'd be
happy to listen to them."

Kirk followed the bishop around the building as he
checked to make sure all the windows in the classrooms
were closed. "You're asking me?" Kirk asked.

"Yes, if you don't mind. I'm a convert, so I didn't have
the benefit of growing up in the Church. And before I was
called to be bishop, the only other church job I'd ever had
was serving as the financial clerk. Also, my oldest child is
only eight years old, so I don't have much experience with
people your age."

"But you were my age once, so it's not like you don't
know anything about it."

"I spent most of my time studying math and science."
Kirk was disappointed. "Oh."

"Before you moved into the ward, there was just
Jonathan. I was more like him when I was growing up. But
now that you're here, I think we need to work on building
a priests quorum. We have a few inactives we might get to
come out. So, as you can see, your coming here has been
very important."

"Actually, though, I might not be staying here." It was
the first time Kirk had told anyone.

"Where would you go?"

"Back home. I've been talking to one of my friends in
Idaho. He thinks that as soon as his brother leaves on a
mission, he can talk his parents into letting me come and
stay with them."

"Have you talked to your folks about this?" Bishop
Merrill asked.

"Not yet, but I will as soon as my friend's parents say
it's okay for me to move in with them."

"I see. Well, we can sure use you here, but I can see
why you'd want to go back where everybody knows you."

"I feel bad for abandoning you, but to tell you the
truth, I don't think you can have much of a quorum with
only two guys who don't have anything in common."

The bishop locked the outside door on their way out.
There was only one car left in the parking lot. The bishop
drove a plain, late-model economy car. Kirk felt it matched
his personality—it did the job with as little fanfare as possible.

"Would you mind if we stop somewhere for a moment
on the way?" the bishop asked. "I need to drop by a key to
our new ward librarian. It will just take a minute."

"Yeah, sure."

"Do you know Sister Watson?"

"No."

"Her husband passed away in March, just after he retired. She's been having kind of a hard time adjusting to being all alone. I like to stop in once in a while. Today we sustained her to be the ward librarian. That'll keep her working with a lot of people. I think she needs that right now." They pulled into a driveway. "Would you like to come in and meet her?"

"I guess so."

Sister Watson opened the door before they had a chance to ring the bell. She greeted them both with a warm smile.

"I brought you the key to the library," Bishop Merrill said.

"Oh, Bishop, you didn't need to go out of your way for that," Sister Watson said.

"We were in the neighborhood anyway. Do you know Kirk?"

She turned to Kirk. "Well, of course. You help bless the sacrament every week, don't you? You do a good job."

Kirk dropped his gaze and mumbled thanks.

"Won't you both come in?" Sister Watson asked.

"Well, maybe, but just for a minute," the bishop said.

It was a small house in an old part of town. On the wall were family pictures showing three children as they grew up.

"Is there anything you need done around the house?" Bishop Merrill asked.

"No, I'm doing just fine."

"On our way out, would it be all right if Kirk and I take a peek in your backyard? We're always looking for service projects for our youth, you know."

"I think everything is in pretty good shape, but you're welcome to look around."

A few minutes later the bishop and Kirk took a tour of Sister Watson's backyard. Back in the car, as he was driving Kirk home, the bishop said, "Did you notice her fence?"

"Her fence?"

"It needs to be painted."

"I didn't think it was very bad."

"I saw some bare spots. As a member of the priests quorum, are you content to let it stay that way over the winter?"

"What priests quorum? We only have two people. Maybe her home teachers could paint the fence."

"Her home teachers are only two people also. Besides, they've been mowing her lawn all summer."

"Why don't you just come out and say it—you want me and Jonathan to paint her fence?"

The bishop smiled. "All right. I want you and Jonathan to paint her fence."

"Oh, man," Kirk complained. "She probably doesn't even know her fence needs painting."

"But we know, don't we? And if some of that wood is exposed to the wind and the snow, it will end up being destroyed."

"It's not a very good fence, anyway," Kirk said.

"Maybe not, but it's the only fence she's got."

"What if she can't afford the paint?" Kirk said.

"Let me worry about that."

Kirk looked at the bishop with suspicion. "You knew about her fence before we went there, didn't you?"

The bishop turned away to hide a smile. "Will Saturday morning be okay for you? I'll be able to help out then."

"I guess so."

"Will you call Jonathan and see if he can do it then too?"

"All right, but you've got to promise you won't let him sing."

That afternoon Kirk got a phone call from Chad Davis, his best friend back home in Idaho. "I talked to my parents. They said it's okay if you come out here and live with us during your junior and senior years. My brother goes into the MTC a week from Wednesday, so anytime after that'd be good."

"I'll be there."

"Have you talked to your folks about it?" Chad asked.

"Not yet. I'll do it right after I hang up."

"You think they'll let you?" Chad asked.

"I hope so. They know I'm not very happy here."

His discussion with his parents went better than he'd hoped. At first his mother said it was out of the question, that she wasn't ready to give him up so soon. But his dad knew how important it was to Kirk and avoided giving a quick decision. "We need to talk about this."

Kirk did his best to answer each of their concerns. He promised to live the same standards there as he would if he were at home. And if he failed to live up to his end of the agreement, he agreed to return to live with his parents.

At the end of their discussion, his dad said, "I guess this is something you need to decide for yourself, Kirk. We'll support you, whatever you decide."

Kirk said he'd pray about it and think about it seriously, but as soon as he left his parents, he privately called Chad and told him he would soon be coming to live with Chad's family.

On Monday morning school was no longer something to dread. Kirk told himself that it didn't matter because he wasn't going to stay in Nebraska anyway.

When he came out of his eleven o'clock class, on his

way to the cafeteria for lunch, he saw Boone Gideon, the school Goliath, shove Jonathan hard against the lockers. "I'm going to kill you, you little . . . " Boone said.

"Is there a problem here?" Kirk asked, walking up to Boone.

"I'm going to kill him, that's the problem," Boone said.

Kirk shook his head. "I don't think so."

Boone let go of Jonathan and turned to face Kirk. "You gonna stop me?"

Kirk wasn't sure how he'd do against Boone in a fight, but people were watching to see what he'd do, so he felt like he couldn't back down. Besides, even if he was thrown out of school for fighting, it didn't matter because he was leaving anyway. "I'm not going to let you pick on him."

"Let's take this outside then," Boone grumbled.

They went outside to a secluded area in back of the school. About twenty people followed them because they wanted to see a good fight. Even Jonathan went along with the crowd.

Kirk felt an adrenaline rush. He wondered what his face would look like when they were done. Boone was bigger than Kirk. He only hoped Boone was slower. If he was, Kirk would do okay.

Kirk and Boone circled around each other, their fists up, looking for an excuse to begin pummeling each other.

"How come you're so mad at Jonathan anyway?" Kirk asked.

"I sit next to him in class."

"Yeah? So?"

"So he hums songs all through class."

Kirk dropped his guard. "He hums?"

"You heard me. He hums. All the time. One stupid song after another. It's driving me crazy."

Kirk turned to Jonathan. "Jonathan, you can't go

around humming in class. If you hummed around me, I'd want to punch you out too."

"Most of the time I don't even know I'm doing it."

"Boone, look, he's sorry he hummed. Aren't you, Jonathan?"

"Yeah, sure. What was I humming anyway?"

"How should I know what you were humming?" Boone snapped.

"It was probably from *Phantom of the Opera,*" Jonathan said as he started to hum one of the songs from the musical.

"You're doing it again!" Kirk shouted.

"I know I was. I was just wondering if either one of you can identify what musical it's from?"

Kirk grabbed Jonathan by the collar and pulled him close to him. Speaking slowly and distinctly, he said, "You'd better say you're sorry you hummed, Jonathan, or else Boone and I are *both* going to punch you out."

Finally Jonathan realized he was in danger. "Sorry."

Kirk turned to Boone. "He said he's sorry."

"Why were you sticking up for him, anyway?"

"I'm Jonathan's . . . uh . . . acquaintance."

"Are you into singing too?"

"What, are you crazy?"

Boone was satisfied. "Good."

The confrontation was over. Kirk and Boone walked back into the school and ate lunch together. Kirk wasn't sure who Jonathan ate with.

On Saturday morning Bishop Merrill picked Kirk and Jonathan up at eight-thirty, so they could get an early start on Sister Watson's fence.

"I'll take care of sanding and you two do the painting," the bishop said.

It seemed fair enough at first. But as they were

unloading supplies from the bishop's trunk, Kirk noticed two paint brushes, a power sander, and a long extension cord.

The bishop finished sanding the worst parts of the fence by ten o'clock. "Well, I'm done, but I'll stick around and give you guys moral support."

"You could paint too," Kirk suggested.

"There're only two brushes."

"You could go get another brush."

"Too expensive," the bishop said. Then he went to the back door and asked Sister Watson if she had a lawn chair he could use. A few minutes later he was set up with a lawn chair, a pitcher of lemonade, and some donuts she'd bought for them.

"These are great donuts," he said. "You'll really like them when you take a break."

"When will that be?" Jonathan asked.

"After you finish the side you're working on."

It was a great day to be outside, the first really warm day they'd had for a week. At first it was hard to get into the work. Kirk felt lazy and using the heavy brush soon made his wrist and arm ache. But he was surprised by how hard Jonathan worked. They started on opposite ends of the fence and painted toward each other. Kirk was determined not to let Jonathan out-paint him, so the work went pretty fast.

After a while, Bishop Merrill asked, "Kirk, have you read the scriptures I gave you last Sunday?"

"Not yet."

"Well, that's okay, I can read them to you. Save you some time later on. I'll go get my scriptures and be right back."

While he was gone, Kirk said to Jonathan, "I'm not sure, but I think we've been set up."

"What do you mean?"

"I mean this whole thing isn't about painting a fence."

"Really? What's it about?"

"He's trying to teach us something."

"What?"

"I don't know yet."

"That reminds me of a song."

"Don't push it, Jonathan. I have a loaded paint brush in my hand."

"Sorry."

Bishop Merrill returned to his lawn chair and opened his scriptures. "I really like the passage in the Book of Mormon that talks about the sacrament. It's in Third Nephi. Here, I'll read it for you."

He began reading. *And when the disciples had come with bread and wine, he took of the bread and brake and blessed it; and he gave unto the disciples and commanded that they should eat. And when they had eaten and were filled, he commanded that they should give unto the multitude. And when the multitude had eaten and were filled, he said unto the disciples: Behold there shall one be ordained among you, and to him will I give power that he shall break bread and bless it and give it unto the people of my church, unto all those who shall believe and be baptized in my name. And this shall ye always observe to do, even as I have done, even as I have broken bread and blessed it and given it unto you. And this shall ye do in remembrance of my body, which I have shown unto you. And it shall be a testimony unto the Father that ye do always remember me. And if ye do always remember me ye shall have my Spirit to be with you.*

The bishop stopped reading. The only nearby sounds were the rhythmic slapping of two brushes on the fence and the singing of a few birds. Down the street someone was running a lawn mower.

"Why do you think he wants us to always remember him?" Bishop Merrill asked.

"So we'll think about what he did for us," Jonathan said.

"Yes. Any other reasons?"

Kirk realized it had been a long time since he'd thought about things like this. "So we can try to be more like him."

"Very good. I think the Savior is pleased to know of the service you two are giving today," Bishop Merrill said. "I found something the other day in the footnotes of the New Testament that I'd never noticed before. It's in Mark, chapter seven." The bishop found the page he wanted. "Apparently the Savior had gone into a house to rest up from all the throngs of people who followed him wherever he went. The people found out where he was and they rushed to the house. He was exhausted. The Joseph Smith translation says, *and would that no man should come unto him. But he could not deny them; for he had compassion upon all men.*"

The bishop left to run an errand, promising to be back to help finish up, and so they were left to their own thoughts.

Kirk knew it wouldn't last, but for one brief moment, as he moved the paint brush up and down the slats of the picket fence, and even with the sound of Jonathan humming some Church song, he felt deep love and gratitude for Jesus Christ.

They finished around noon. The best part of the day was when they escorted Sister Watson outside to see what they had done. Kirk tried not to show it, but he felt really great as she looked at the newly painted fence. "Oh, this is so wonderful! You dear boys, you dear, sweet boys. I can't believe you'd do this for me."

On the way home, the bishop dropped Jonathan off first and then took Kirk home. When they pulled into the driveway, he turned to Kirk and said, "If you decide to stay here, I'd like to call you to serve as the first assistant in the priests quorum."

Kirk was having second thoughts about his decision to return to Idaho. "Is it okay if I let you know tomorrow?"

"Yes, of course. You did a good job today, Kirk. I'm proud of you."

The next day, as sacrament meeting was about to begin, Jonathan and Kirk were once again sitting at the sacrament table.

During the prelude music, Kirk looked into the congregation and saw Sister Watson. She caught his eye and gave him a warm smile.

Kirk wondered what it was like for her to have her husband gone after so many years. Kirk wondered, too, who in the congregation might have a special need to partake of the sacrament that day.

A few minutes later, the sacrament hymn began. Kirk and Jonathan stood up, folded back the white linen cloth, and began to break the bread.

Because there were so many priests in his quorum in Idaho, Kirk had seldom been assigned to bless the sacrament in his own ward. Here, in Nebraska, he and Jonathan had the assignment every week.

This time it was different. This time he tried to imagine the Savior's hands tearing the original loaf—strong hands, the hands of a carpenter accustomed to working hard with wood, but they were also hands that had touched the sick and dying and brought them back to health. Those same hands were later pierced with nails when he was crucified.

Jonathan offered the sacrament prayer on the bread. Somehow his voice wasn't as irritating to Kirk as usual. He read the simple prayer sincerely and with some feeling.

After the prayer, Jonathan stood up and together he and Kirk handed out the four gleaming trays to the deacons. The two priests continued to stand until the deacons were in place, then they sat down.

Kirk looked out at the congregation. Most people sat quietly with their heads down, avoiding eye contact with anyone, deep in their private thoughts.

A few minutes later the deacons brought the trays back. Jonathan and Kirk each partook of the bread, accepted the trays from the deacons, and served the younger boys. Then the two priests set the trays back on the table and folded back the cloth to reveal the four water trays, all in a neat, precise line.

Kirk knelt down. He looked at the words of the sacrament prayer. *These are the words of the Savior,* he thought. *This is what he wants me to say. Maybe doing this will help someone today. Maybe it will help Sister Watson.*

Kirk tried to picture what it was like when the Savior instituted the sacrament just hours before he was arrested. The Savior held that simple cup in his hands, blessed its contents, then passed it to one of the apostles, who drank of it and then passed it on. The Savior's hands . . . the Savior's words.

"Oh God, the Eternal Father . . . "

Minutes later, as the deacons passed the sacrament tray from row to row, Kirk watched as Sister Watson took the cup and drank it. He was glad to have had a part in providing the sacrament to her.

In the time remaining until the deacons returned, Kirk tried to imagine what it had been like for the Savior to be hanging on that cross, feeling the pain of the nails and the difficulty of breathing in the position he was in, feeling the humiliation of being made a roadside attraction for travelers to stare at as they passed. Did Jesus search the

crowd for sympathetic faces? Where were the ones he had
healed? He had been there for them—why weren't they
there when he needed them?

The mother of Jesus had been there, though. Kirk realized how devastated the Savior must have been that his
mother had to see him being tortured by cruel men.

Some in the crowd openly made fun of the Savior and
mocked him and, with sneers on their faces, challenged
him to come down from the cross, saying that then they'd
believe him.

Kirk looked down at his own hands. They had just
acted in behalf of the Savior's hands. *What kind of hands are
mine?* he thought. Nothing special. Just hands. He noticed
a few specks of paint remained under his fingernails.

His hands . . . my hands. I need to be careful.

After the deacons returned with the nearly empty
trays, Kirk and Jonathan partook of the sacrament, served
the deacons, returned each tray to the table, and folded
back the cloth over it all. Then, after being excused by the
bishop, they went to sit with their families.

When sacrament meeting was over, Kirk wanted to see
the bishop, so he told his parents to go on home without
him. He waited in the hall for the bishop to finish his
interviews.

At one-thirty the bishop was done and invited Kirk
into his office.

"I've decided I'm going to stay here," Kirk said.

"Really? Are you sure?"

"I'm sure."

"What made you change your mind?"

"Yesterday . . . and today."

"You want to tell me about it?"

Kirk turned his palms up and brought his hands up to
belt level and looked down at them. He realized that if he

tried to say what he had felt during the sacrament, he would lose control, and he was afraid of that. "Maybe some other time, okay?"

"Of course. Can I give you a ride home?"

On the way home, Kirk started to feel bad that he was not going to be hiking and camping with his friends in the priests quorum back in his old ward in Idaho. He couldn't just let it go. He had to say something. "Bishop, would it kill you to camp out with the priests sometime?"

"Well, no, I could camp with you and Jonathan. We could go somewhere next summer."

"I was thinking maybe we could do some winter camping."

The bishop's eyes got big. "You mean in the snow?"

"Sure, why not? It's not that bad, really. You might even like it."

"Well, I don't know. I've never done any camping in the snow."

"I know that . . . but . . . you *are* the president of the priests quorum." It made him smile inside to say it.

The bishop swallowed hard. "All right, come up with a plan and present it next week. We'll see what Jonathan says. If Jonathan wants to go outside during some blizzard and risk his life, well, we'll do it."

Kirk realized the bishop was counting on Jonathan to kill the idea. But Kirk had a plan of his own. "I'm pretty sure he'll go along with it if I promise him we'll sing songs by the campfire."

The bishop suppressed a grin. "I wonder who's going to get to him first, me or you?"

"I am. Jonathan owes me a favor."

They pulled into Kirk's driveway. "This is going to be okay, Bishop." Kirk opened the car door, then said, "I think I might learn a lot from you."

The bishop leaned over to look at Kirk, who had gotten out of the car and was standing next to it. "I'll learn a lot from you too."

"Even if we don't go camping, it'll be okay," Kirk responded.

"Really, why's that?"

"Because we're going to be a quorum."

On his way in to tell his parents he had decided to stay home instead of moving back to Idaho, Kirk caught himself humming a tune. He realized it was from *Phantom of the Opera.*